Single Bells
Joan Donaldson-Yarmey

- and -

Gwen Donaldson

Print ISBNs
Amazon Print 9780228628378
Ingram Spark 9780228628385
BWL Print 9780228628392

http://bwlpublishing.ca

Dedication

To Bob G. A Very Dear Friend

Table of Contents

6

Chapter One

Simone Bell-Watson looked up as Raymond Webster of the Webster Private Detective Agency entered her office. He walked up to her desk and set a brown manila envelope on it. The envelope had her first name printed in capital letters on the front. Raymond then went to the coffee corner and put a pod of coffee in the top of the machine and closed the lid. He pushed the button to start it.

Simone looked down at the envelope in front of her. Did she want to open it? She'd hired Raymond Webster three weeks ago to follow her husband, Griffin. Six months ago Griffin had claimed to have made new friends and began spending time with them going to hockey games, bars, or just having coffee. But he was never able to describe the games they went to and he'd never brought his new friends to the house.

"Would you like me to summarize my report or do you want to read it?" Raymond asked as he carried his paper cup of coffee to the chair in front of her desk. He was in his early fifties with salt and pepper hair worn in a type of crew cut that was three centimetres long at the top and tapered on the sides. He had on blue jeans and a black leather jacket, which seemed to be the typical outfit of private detectives on television.

Instead of answering, Simone turned the envelope over and lifted the flap. She reached in and pulled out three sheets of paper and two large, coloured photographs. She spread them out on her desk and gasped in shock. She stared at the pictures for a long time before finally picking them up, one in each hand. The first was typical of the type you saw on television detective shows where the spouse is kissing another person in front of a motel door. The other one was Griffin and a man climbing out of the back seat of a car half dressed. Both were laughing. It was at night and looked like they were in a deserted parking lot.

"That was taken in Stanley Park. I had followed the man there and used a Nikon night vision camera."

Simone blinked back the tears. It was true. Griffin was having an affair, something she'd suspected while at the same time not really believing he would do that to her, to their marriage. What she hadn't imagined or expected was that it would be with another man.

"As you know, it has taken me a long time to finally get these pictures," Raymond said. "He must have been suspicious that someone was watching him because whenever I tried to follow him he would make quick turns and drive through different neighbourhoods never stopping anywhere. It was really impossible for me to keep up with him and still not be noticed. I lost him many times. So I tried a different tactic."

Raymond took a sip of his coffee. "I began watching the women at his work place but nothing seemed to be going on there. Then I sat and watched the women in your neighbourhood. Again, nothing." He paused. "I finally decided to watch the men."

Simone studied the pictures. She didn't recognize the man.

"This one always seemed to leave his house at the same time as your husband. So I followed him. He wasn't as wary as your husband and drove straight to the park that night."

Simone set the photographs down and picked up the report. It gave an itemized account of what Raymond had done each evening that he had followed Griffin or the days he had watched Griffin's work place. She read them through, remembering the excuses Griffin had given for leaving the house.

"I need some cigarettes and beer."

"I'm meeting my friends at a bar for some drinks."

At the bottom of the third page was the total amount she owed.

Simone took a deep breath. "Would you like a cheque or an e-transfer?"

"E-transfer is fine."

Raymond gave her his email address and she went on her cell phone and made the payment.

"If you ever need me again, just give me a call." Raymond set his cup on her desk and left the room.

Simone stared down at the pictures. She and Griffin had been married three years and, until six months ago, she had thought it was a good marriage. Then he had made new friends and began to change. He shaved before going out and he talked about getting hair transplants for his thinning crown. She had recognized those changes as signs that he may have someone new in his life, someone he wanted to impress. And she'd just been proven right.

She didn't know why she was more stunned Griffin was having an affair with a man than she might have been if he'd been seeing a woman. It wasn't such an uncommon occurrence anymore. There were even shows about it, shows like *Frankie and Grace* starring Lily Tomlin, Jane Fonda, Sam Waterston, and Martin Sheen. They had been two couples for years and then the men finally admitted that they had fallen in love. The women had taken it hard and then tried to get on with their lives. With her blonde hair, medium height, and blue eyes she wasn't as sophisticated as Jane Fonda's character or as off the wall as Lilly Tomlin's but she may have to watch old episodes of the show to see how they worked their way to their new normal.

Well, it was time to put her back-up plan to work for, in spite of her hopes, deep in her mind she'd known what the result would be—Griffin was seeing someone else. And she had prepared for that.

Simone picked up her phone and dialed a number. "This is Simone Bell-Watson. I'd like to take that storage unit we discussed and I will be bringing my furniture in this afternoon."

While waiting for the person on the other end to agree, Simone decided she would have to get busy and change the name on her important papers back to Bell.

"We're open until six this evening."

"Thank you." Simone hung up and dialed another number. "I'm Simone Bell-Watson. I phoned last week about possibly needing your services to move my furniture."

"Yes, I remember you," the woman on the other end said.

"I'd like your men and truck to be at my place at one o'clock this afternoon."

"Just a minute while I check our schedule."

Simone stared at the wall while she waited. She wasn't sure what was harder to take, losing a husband to a heart attack at the age of thirty-seven or having a husband cheat on her. Both meant a loss of a marriage, of a lifestyle, and of a planned future with a man. She and her first husband, Lucas, had met when she was nineteen and had dated for two years before marrying. That had lasted until his death seven years later. It had taken her two years before she began dating again and had met Griffin. For a second time she'd fallen in love and looked forward to a long marriage.

"I can arrange for a crew to meet you at one o'clock."

Simone was startled out of her reverie and brought back to the present. "Thank you."

After Simone had given her address, she made one more phone call. This one she dreaded but it was necessary for, while she'd made plans for moving out if necessary, she'd left this one until the last possible moment.

"Hello, Simone," a woman's voice said.

"Hi, Mom. I'll get right to the point. I need a place to stay for a while."

"So, you're finally leaving that ne'er-do-well."

"Ne'er do well? Why do you keep using those old words?" Her mother, Patricia Reed-Bell, was a very successful, historical romance writer who liked to add little-used and archaic words to her speech. She had just turned seventy and had been a widow since the death of Simone's father, Craig, almost two years ago.

"Because they have a lot more flair and elegance than today's words," Patricia said. "Lazy and shiftless just doesn't express the same righteous indignation. Although, Griffin was certainly lazy and shiftless. So what did he do that finally made you to come to your senses?"

Simone thought about lying and saying that she'd been the one having an affair and decided to leave him, but she knew the truth would come out. After all, she couldn't tell that to her and Griffin's friends. She wondered if some of them already suspected he'd been screwing around on her. She knew people automatically suspected an affair if they saw a married man or woman out with someone of the opposite sex. Would her friends have thought an affair if they saw Griffin out with a man? She knew she wouldn't if she'd seen one of their husbands with another man. She'd have thought it was a couple of buddies having a drink.

"Griffin is seeing someone." She couldn't bring herself to tell the whole truth just yet.

There was quiet on the other end. "I'm sorry to hear that," Patricia finally said.

"I have to go and pack my things." Simone didn't want to talk about how she had found out right now.

"I'll have Lauren put one more plate on the table for dinner."

Lauren Huckley had been hired part-time by Patricia to look after Craig when he'd had his first stroke three years ago. When Craig died from a second stroke Lauren had continued to come in three days a week to clean and cook. But Patricia enjoyed her company, so last July had hired her full time and Lauren had moved into the house. She didn't have a car and used Patricia's whenever they went out or she needed to go shopping.

"I'm not sure what time I'll get there."

"We'll keep it warm for you."

Simone hung up and sat looking at the pictures. She wasn't sure if she was angrier at being such a fool, or more hurt that he had lied to her, or more embarrassed that she'd had to hire a private investigator. She'd been in love with Griffin since their second date, but she'd also known that he wasn't ready to settle down. While they dated she continued with the studies she'd started after Lucas died and had received her Bachelor's degree in English literature. After hearing for years how her mother's literary agent had worked hard to find the right publishing house for her manuscripts and had gotten her many lucrative deals, Simone had decided she wanted to become a literary agent. There weren't any requirements such as training, exams, or certifications to become an agent but she knew she had to gain experience. She worked as an assistant at a publishing company to learn the ins and outs of the publishing industry. She found that it took hard work and determination to be an agent but the most important thing she learned was the art of negotiation. After two years she started her own agency.

She began by working out of her home using the inheritance money she'd received from her grandmother to live on. She built up a stable of clients and found publishers to work with. Finally, last year she'd rented an office, put Bell Literary Agency on the door, and hired two agents.

Just when Simone was about to pop the question herself, Griffin finally asked her to marry him. At the time, she hadn't been sure if that was because he wanted to get married or because he was tired of her hanging around waiting for the question to be asked. She had even thought it might have been because her company was growing and she was earning good money. Now, she wondered if it was because he hadn't been able to admit his sexual preference and had wanted to hide in their marriage.

She'd thought he was a good husband, although not very ambitious. He'd been working in a warehouse when they met and he was still doing the exact same job now. They seldom argued and while they also seldom hugged or kissed and the sex had been sparse, she was happy in their marriage. Looking back now, she realized they were more like housemates instead of lovers. But she'd thought that in spite of their lack of lovemaking he was at least faithful. Now that had proven to be false. And being unfaithful was a deal breaker for her whether it was with a woman or a man.

Simone wiped a tear from her eye. Her marriage was over and nothing would change that. She was closing in on forty and alone again. Probably would be for the rest of her life.

Rather than phone her younger sister, Simone sent a text telling Serena that she was leaving Griffin and would be transferring her things out of the condo and into storage and moving in with their mother. Then she shut off her phone. She didn't need to go through the whole explanation right now.

Simone picked up the envelope, stood, and went around her desk. She took her coat off the coat rack and put it on. She opened the door to the outer office where her secretary, Grace, was typing on her keyboard.

It was the first week of December and the room had a decorated Christmas tree in one corner and lights around the outer door. Holiday music played softly through the open door of the office across hers which was shared by her two agents. She could see Jilly on the phone and Ramona reading on her computer screen through the doorway.

"I'll be gone for the rest of the day." Simone told Grace.

"But you have a client coming in to discuss his new manuscript." Grace was dressed in jeans and a red sweater with a reindeer brooch on the shoulder. There were matching reindeer earrings in her ears. She'd been dressing in red or green outfits since December first.

"Give him my apologies and reschedule for tomorrow or the next day, which ever suits him," Simone said. She'd worked hard to grow her literary agency and always tried to be available for her clients. But what she had to do was more important. And she had to work fast at packing up her clothes and dishes and bedding and everything else in the condo. Griffin got off work at five. "And I will have my phone off until tomorrow, so just leave me a message."

Grace nodded.

Simone went over to the photocopier to make two copies of each of the pictures Raymond Webster had given her. She felt Grace watching her since photocopying was part of her job, but these pictures were something Simone didn't want to share with everyone. She put the original and copies in the envelope and hurried down to her bright red Mercedes car in the underground parkade. She drove out onto the street. It was half snowing/half raining, which wasn't unusual for Vancouver this time of year. If she wasn't so hurt and angry the snow might have put her in the Christmas spirit.

Simone drove to the condo she and Griffin shared. It was on the second floor of the building and overlooked the city and the mountains in the distance. She loved the view and would miss it. They wouldn't have any trouble selling it unless Griffin wanted to buy her out. She snorted at the idea. In their three years of marriage Griffin hadn't looked for a better paying job. She wasn't sure if that was because he really liked his work or because he didn't care about growing and expanding his prospects. The monthly condo payments and fees, groceries, and utilities were paid out of their joint account but her deposits were larger than his. And he had only come up with one-third of the condo down payment. She had kept the paperwork to prove it.

* * *

Serena Bell set down the bill of lading for the shipment of beer that had been delivered to her pub that morning on her desk and looked at the text from her sister. She read it twice before actually believing it. Then she nodded in satisfaction. Simone had finally smartened up and was leaving Griffin. Serena had never liked the man, finding him lazy and basically willing to live off his wife.

Serena decided to go to Simone's condo. She figured there was no use wasting this opportunity to help get her sister away from that man. Also, it would be a chance to find out what had happened that would cause her to leave the man she had waited so long to marry. It must have been something drastic to cause Simone to decide to move in with their mother.

She finished up some paperwork then picked up her purse and keys and hurried out into the main lounge area. She'd owned this pub for just over a year and she still got a thrill to look around and realize it belonged to her. She'd spent most of her twenties working as a salesperson in a department store, or a server in a restaurant or, after getting her mixology license, a bartender in a bar or pub. These jobs lasted long enough for her to save some money and then she travelled throughout Canada and the United States for as long as the money lasted. While working in the bars she'd enjoyed mixing drinks for her customers and had learned a few easy, flair techniques, like the basic flip, ice throwing, and the palm pivot. They weren't as easy as they looked but she'd perfected them through much practice.

Then two years ago she'd decided it was time to grow up so she'd bought the original bar here in Richmond using the inheritance she, Simone, and four other grandchildren had received from their grandmother. At the same time, she'd put a down payment on one of the condos above it.

But she knew that owning a bar wasn't for her. She didn't like the racket of the music and loud conversation or having to deal with the drunks or put up with the groping hands of some of the customers.

When she started looking for some place to buy she'd learned that the difference between a pub and a bar was that bars are all about selling alcohol. They served beer, a wide selection of cocktails, and not much in the way of food, usually snacks or appetizers. Bars targeted a specific market. That's why there were many different types like, sports bars, ladies bars, and gay bars.

Pubs were half way between a bar and a restaurant. They didn't target an audience; they were open to anyone and everyone. They served beer, wine, and cider and had a full menu of food from breakfast to desserts. Because of the wide variety of food and little liquor, minors were allowed in as long as accompanied by an adult.

So she'd made some changes to the original business. She renovated the kitchen to increase efficiency and flow, expanded the menu to include more choices, and updated the front of the house, as the area where she and her staff interacted with customers was called. She knew that first impressions were very important, so she enlarged the entranceway and added a comfortable couch for waiting customers or ones who had come to pick up an order to sit on. She also placed menus on a small shelf in the corner so they had something to read while waiting.

She made sure the hostess station was visible from the door, as well as from the rest of the room. That way anyone of the staff could greet the customers as soon as they entered. She kept the menus on the podium, handy for the server to pick up while leading the customers to a table or booth.

Most importantly, she changed the name to the B&B Pub. The name was a conversation starter with the customers and always got a laugh when she explained its origin. In school she and Simone had called themselves the BB sisters or the BB Bells: BB standing for Brains and Brawn for Simone because she'd been smart and a tom boy. Serena was Brains and Beauty. She made high grades in her classes and had also been beautiful, winning two minor beauty pageants in her teens. Since then, she'd put on a little weight and cut her long, blonde hair short. She was two years younger than Simone and just an inch shorter.

Lenny Newman, her beverage server/waiter, was behind the counter. She walked up to him.

"I'll be gone for the rest of the day."

"Okay, Boss," Lenny smiled. "I'll take care of everything."

"Thank you. Give me a call if anything comes up."

Serena walked out the front of the B&B Pub and around the corner to the pub parking lot. Past that, at the back of the building, was her metallic blue Prius in the condo parking lot. Traffic was light and it took only half hour to get to her sister's place in Vancouver. There was a large van parked in the front of the building doors and three men were unloading flattened boxes when she arrived. Serena had a key to the building and Simone's condo.

"Where are you men going?"

"We're moving the furniture of a Simone Bell-Watson out of her condo."

She nodded and opened the doors for them. She led them up to the fourth floor condo.

"Serena. What are you doing here?" Simone exclaimed when Serena walked in.

"I've come to help you."

"This could take a while. Aren't you supposed to meet Jerry for dinner tonight?"

Serena waved her hand in dismissal. She had found Jerry online and after six weeks of texting, they had met in person a month ago. Since then she'd seen him twice and the last time hadn't gone well. Jerry had questioned her about her religion and how important it was to her. Once she'd told him she was a Protestant but didn't go to church regularly his texts had slowed. "He called me yesterday and said he had decided to go to Calgary to see his family for Hanukah. I have all day and evening to help you so tell me what to do."

The three men began opening up the folded boxes and taping the bottoms.

"You can pack the dishes I've set on the counter into those boxes, while I show the men what furniture I'm taking with me."

Serena took off her coat and threw it on a kitchen chair. The kitchen, dining room, and living room was all one open area. Down a short hallway were the two bedrooms and a bathroom. Off the living room was a deck where Serena and Simone had spent many an evening drinking wine, talking, and laughing. Serena was going to miss visits with her sister and the view of the city and mountains.

The condo and deck were adorned with Simone's usual abundance of Christmas decorations, although she hadn't put up her tree. Serena knew that Griffin disliked the Christmas fuss and advertising and gift giving, stating that it was only to line the rich people's pockets. He particularly disliked all the decorations Simone put up in their apartment. Serena wondered if Griffin had finally had enough of the Christmas season.

On the counter sat stacks of plates, dessert plates, bowls, and rows of glasses and coffee cups. Serena picked up one of the packing papers and set it on the bottom of a box then set a plate on top. She kept layering the plates, then did the pie plates and bowls. She set the tray of cutlery and other cooking utensils on the bottom of another box and wrapped the glasses and coffee cups in the papers and laid them on top.

While Serena was filling the boxes, the men carried the couch, love seat, ottoman, and end tables out to the van. One of the men smiled at her when he went by. He was the youngest and the tallest of the three and had dark hair shaved on the sides and curly on top, blue eyes, and high cheekbones. She guessed his age to be in the mid-thirties, while the other two were in their forties. He had taken off his jacket and she could see the muscles bulging under his black t-shirt. She returned the smile, feeling a warming sensation in her stomach.

The men hauled the bed, dressers, and night stands from the master bedroom through the living room and out the door. Serena paused and watched them go by. Actually, all of the men were in good shape but the two older men were intent on doing their job. The younger one caught her eye again and winked.

Simone carried plastic garbage bags out of her bedroom and set them against the wall by the door. "These are my clothes and they will go in the back of my car when we leave," she told Serena and the men.

"Where is your furniture going?" Serena asked Simone as she went to the kitchen sink and ran some water into a glass.

"I've rented a storage unit and I'm going to put them there until I figure out where I'm going next."

Serena felt sorry for her sister. Simone had lost one husband to a heart attack and now was losing another to divorce. Serena had never been lucky enough, if lucky was the right word, to find a man she wanted to settle down with. She'd had many lovers and affairs but they had only been a 'passing fancy' as her mother called them.

Serena knew now wasn't the time to ask Simone what had happened between her and Griffin. It looked as if Simone was in a hurry to get everything out of the condo before Griffin came home from work. Serena noticed that Simone was leaving all the furniture in the guest bedroom. She knew that the bed and dresser in it were the only furniture that Griffin had brought into their marriage. The rest had belonged to Simone.

As Serena boxed up cooking and baking ware, the man in the black t-shirt stopped at the counter and slid a piece of paper with his name, Doug, and phone number on it towards her. "Call me," he said then hurried to catch up with the other men.

"Another man falling under your spell?" Simone asked as she took down the Christmas decorations.

Serena laughed. Although they called themselves the BB Bell sisters, their friends had also given them nicknames: Simone with her quick smile, had been known as Tinker Bell because she liked to tinker around on cars with their father. They'd taken an old clunker that she bought with the money she'd saved from her babysitting and part-time job and had fixed it up and painted it. Simone had driven her friends to school football games and to parties in it.

Serena was called Hells Bells by her friends because she was always getting into trouble. There hadn't been a week go by that she wasn't called into the principal's office for some prank she pulled. And because of her beauty she'd been popular with the boys. They would line up in school and beg her for a date causing blockades in the hallways. That usually got her a trip to the principal's office even though she claimed it wasn't her fault. Sometimes, when her sister was gone, Serena would sneak Simone's keys and take her friends for a joy ride. They always pooled their money afterwards and put gas in the tank so Simone wouldn't notice.

"He is kind of cute," Serena said, putting the paper in her purse.

"What about Jerry?" Simone carefully placed the decorations in two boxes.

"I haven't seen him enough to consider it serious. I'm not even sure if we're even dating." She decided to change subjects. She held up the decorations she'd been taking down. "Are you putting those in storage also?" Their mother decorated her house but not as much as Simone was used to.

"I'm taking these to Mom's. Her house needs more than what she puts up.

Serena smiled. Their mother was in for a surprise this holiday season.

"Do you want to come for dinner at Mom's?"

"Oh, it's pretty late to be showing up unexpectedly."

"I'll text her and let her know you'll be joining us. Lauren always makes extra in case she or Mom wants a snack later so I'm sure there's enough food for one more."

* * *

Simone was tired. Her furniture was in her storage unit and she and Serena had driven to their mother's house on Oak Street. They'd unloaded bags of clothes and carried them up to her old bedroom on the second floor. Her boxes of decorations had gone in the basement. Lauren had kept the food she'd prepared warm and she now set it on the table.

"You hired a gumshoe?" Serena asked as she, Simone, Lauren and their mother sat down for their dinner in Patricia's dining room. The room was large with a glass topped table that sat up to eight people and white straight-backed leather chairs. Along one wall was an antique sideboard that had belonged to Patricia's grandmother and above it hung a large rectangle mirror. An archway led into the kitchen and another one on the wall opposite the sideboard let into the living room. The fourth wall had a double patio door that opened onto a deck overlooking the garden area.

"They don't call themselves gumshoes, I've been informed," Simone said as she dished up some scalloped potatoes. "At one time that cliché probably fit because the private detectives wore street shoes with thick, rubber soles so they could walk softly. Now they wear all types of footwear and have more sophisticated ways of tracking someone."

"So what all did the detective do? How did he find out Griffin was cheating?"

Simone grimaced at the word cheating but she had decided to answer all their questions and get it over with. "Raymond Webster of the Webster Private Detective Agency tried to follow him, but he kept evading him. Finally Mr. Webster watched the women where Griffin worked and in our neighbourhood. When nothing developed there he started looking at the men. He noticed that one of our neighbours left his house around the same time that Griffin left ours. He followed him and found them together."

Simone took a drink of her wine and didn't watch them as the news sunk in.

"Oh," Patricia said.

"Really?" was Serena's reaction. "For sure? And he got pictures?"

Lauren said nothing.

Simone nodded in answer to Serena's question. Before she'd left the condo, she'd spread the photographs on the counter and left them for Griffin. That was all the explanation he would get from her. It should be all the explanation he needed.

"And you never suspected he was gay?" Serena asked.

"No."

"Really?" Serena and Patricia exchanged glances.

"Why? Did you?" Simone stared from her sister to her mother.

"Well," Patricia said slowly. "We did wonder."

"Why?" Simone asked again. "What did he do?"

"Oh, it was nothing overt," Serena said. "Just some of his mannerism, like the way he occasionally waved his hand or struck a pose. Until today, though, if I'd been asked if I truly thought he was gay. I would have said no."

Simone couldn't believe that she had missed the signs. Had she been so much in love with him that she'd refused to acknowledge them? Had she thought her love would keep him at her side?

"Are you going to take some time off?" Patricia asked.

Simone was jerked from her thoughts. "No time off. I'll be back in the office tomorrow, right after I see a lawyer and a real estate agent."

"Good for you, Dear. No use dwelling on times of yore. And you can stay here as long as you need."

"Thank you, Mom." She smiled at her mother.

Patricia was a small, pretty woman with dark hair. She stood barely five foot two inches and had only reached their father's chest when standing beside him. Simone and Serena had taken after Craig in height and with their blonde hair.

Simone looked at Lauren wondering why she was so quiet. Usually she kept them laughing by telling them about the antics she and their mother had gotten into since their last visit. Maybe she was quiet because of the reason Simone was moving in. Maybe she thought it was too sombre an occasion for levity.

"Anything new happen since the last time we saw you two?" Simone asked looking from her mother to Lauren.

"We went to a Christmas craft sale and bought some candles and scented soap," Lauren said. She was medium height with long brown hair that she kept in a ponytail or braids. She was in her mid-forties and had been married once. Her parents were still alive and she had one sister.

Patricia nodded. "And we also went shopping for gifts." She added with a smile.

"Oh!" Serena exclaimed bouncing up and down in her chair. "What did you buy us? What did you buy us?"

Simone remembered the two of them pestering their parents with that same question every year when they were children.

"Nothing for either of you," Patricia said, a sparkle in her eye. "You're both on the naughty list."

Simone laughed for the first time that day. That had also been her mother's reaction to their question every year.

"Oh," Serena pouted then she brightened. "Christmas isn't here yet. I have plenty of time to find out. And speaking of Christmas, it's time to get in the spirit. I'm going to see the lights at the VanDusen Gardens one evening next week. Anyone want to join me?"

"I haven't been there since Mom and Dad took us as kids," Simone said. "I'll go with you." She wanted to start doing some Christmas activities. The news about Griffin had put a damper on her mood but she didn't want to let it spoil the season. She knew there was no way they would ever get back together. If Griffin had been seeing a woman, he could say he'd made a mistake and wanted another chance. But he couldn't change his sexual orientation. She knew she would have sad days, but she also knew it was definitely over.

"Me, too," Patricia said.

They all looked at Lauren. "I'll go, too," she smiled.

Chapter Two

The next morning, Simone lay in bed and stared at the ceiling. Her room hadn't changed much from when she moved out over fifteen years ago. The walls were the same light mauve that she'd insisted she wanted when her father decided it was time to paint them. The double bed had been her parents until they'd purchased a queen-sized one. They had bought her a new flowered quilt with matching shams to go on it which were still on the bed. Her old desk was under the window and the white dressers were still in place, one in the corner and the other one, with a mirror, along the wall opposite the walk-in closet. The door to the ensuite was to the right of the closet. The familiarity of the room had been a comfort last night when she couldn't sleep.

Simone picked up her phone and looked at the blank screen. It had been a tough night. As much as she was angry at Griffin and hurt at his betrayal, she still was surprised that her love for him hadn't diminished much. She'd missed having him beside her in bed and had thought about their vacations to exotic locations where they'd hiked through rainforests, kayaked down rivers, and swam with dolphins. They'd rented a catamaran for two summers with friends and gone sailing on the ocean. In the winters, they'd leased a chalet in Whistler with those same friends and gone downhill skiing most weekends. She wondered if Griffin had let those friends know yet. Or was it up to her?

Simone also wondered how Griffin had slept in their condo alone. Had he thought about all the house hunting they had done together when looking for a place to buy? They'd gone to open houses, met with real estate agents, and even checked for private sales. It had been fun walking through houses, condos, and townhouses, petting cats and talking with dogs that were confined in their kennels. They discussed the number of bedrooms and bathrooms, the layout of the kitchen, dining, and living rooms, the balconies or decks, and if they wanted the extra work of a yard. When they finally signed the papers on their condo, they went out for dinner and celebrated being home owners.

Did sleeping alone in the empty condo bring back any of those memories for him or had he spent the night thinking about his boyfriend? Maybe he'd even invited him over. Making love in a bed would be so much easier and more romantic than in the back seat of a vehicle.

She wondered if he was thinking about their life together. She doubted it; after all, he'd been seeing someone else for months now and had time to deal with the fact that their marriage would soon be over. She was just now discovering it was ending and had to deal with the newness of that.

She pressed the button to turn her cell back on. There was a voicemail from Grace that the writer she had cancelled yesterday would be in this afternoon at two o'clock and a text from her friend, Melanie, wondering if they were still on for drinks this evening.

And there were four phone messages and eleven texts from Griffin.

Simone hesitated then pressed the text icon to see what he'd written.

How did you find out?

I don't think it's right that you took all the furniture.

Where are you staying? With your mother? Your sister?

Simone, I'm sorry. I guess I should have told you.

And then various versions of those four. Simone deleted the voicemails. She didn't need to listen to his voice repeating the same messages. She phoned her office and left Grace a message confirming she'd be there for her two o'clock appointment. She texted Melanie and asked if they could reschedule for some time next week before she shut her phone off again.

After she'd showered and dressed, Simone went downstairs to the kitchen. She smelled coffee brewing and smiled. She needed her coffee this morning. Her mother sat at the table with a full cup and empty plate in front of her.

"Good morning, Simone," Lauren said from the stove. "We're having pancakes this morning. How many would you like?"

"I'll have two." Simone poured herself a cup of coffee and sat down opposite her mother.

"How did you sleep?" Patricia asked.

"Good," Simone lied.

"Must be a load off your shoulders to be rid of him."

Simone hid her grimace behind her coffee cup. Their mother had always spoken her mind but it seemed as she grew older she didn't hold much back.

"What made you suspect something was going on?"

Simone didn't want to get into the whole story. "He began to change, buying new clothes, shaving before going out to meet his friends, spending more time out in the evenings."

"Yes, those are the classic signs. I've written about them enough in my books."

"Are you working on a new one?" Simone smiled her thanks at Lauren as she set a plate with two pancakes in front of her.

"Just finishing the third book of my Regency romance trilogy."

Patricia had been writing as long as Simone could remember. Simone could barely picture the small, two bedroom house they'd first lived in. Patricia was a stay-at-home mom and wanted to be a writer. She would set a clock and tell Simone and Serena that she would be writing for the next half hour and they were supposed to be quiet. They'd play in the living room and as soon as the alarm went off they'd hurry into her parents' bedroom where her mother had set up a small table and computer in one corner. She would hug each of them and then they'd all go back to the living room and play games or have a snack. If the weather was nice they went for a walk to the playground. When they returned Patricia would set the alarm clock and they'd wait until the alarm sounded. Patricia tried to write three or four times a day during the week and half a day on Saturday while their father took them shopping or on some excursion.

And it all paid off. Patricia found an agent for her first book and he got her a contract with a large publishing company. It was an instant success and after three books, Patricia and Craig bought this two storey house with basement on Oak Street. It had a large kitchen, living room, dining room, full bath, and library on the main floor and four bedrooms, all with their own ensuites, on the top floor. There was an extra bedroom, bathroom, family room, and games room in the basement.

The writing routine changed when Simone and Serena started school. Their mother had taken over the library as her office and would write all day. She tried to have finished her daily quota of words before they got home. But sometimes they would walk in the house and see the office door closed. They were never allowed in her office and knew not to disturb her. They would find the snack she had made them and eat it while they waited for her to appear. Sometimes, it would be within a few minutes, occasionally, it would be after their father got home. The three of them would then make dinner and usually their mother would come out in time to eat with them.

"What do you have planned next?" Simone asked her mother.

"Well, I think I'm getting to old to write about young lovers, so I might try something different."

"You told me you're going to try a cozy mystery," Lauren said. "You said you already have ideas for your first two."

"Yes, I might do that. Of course I would write under a pseudonym in case they aren't very popular."

"Well, that's great," Simone said. "Your doctor said that writing is good for your mental health as you grow older. It keeps your mind active and staves off dementia."

Simone stood and put her plate in the dishwasher. "I have a lot to do today." She bent and kissed her mother. "I'll see you both this evening."

On her way to the bank, Simone phoned her lawyer at Cotes and Cotes to make an appointment. Luckily, Anna Cotes had a cancellation and Simone could get in to see her in an hour. It had been too late after putting her furniture in storage yesterday to go to the bank, so she wanted to be there when it opened this morning. She had her own account for her business plus a joint account with Griffin. They had a withdrawal limit of one thousand dollars a day, so she knew Griffin hadn't been able to remove much since last evening.

She was surprised and sadden at how her trust in Griffin had vanished since finding out he'd been cheating on her. Now she didn't know what else to expect from him and wanted to make sure she got her share of their joint account.

The manager was just unlocking the door when she walked up. She smiled and went over to a teller and swiped her card.

"I would like to transfer half of the amount from this joint account into my other account." Simone showed her the business card and swiped it.

Simone had deposited most of the money over their marriage, but she was going to be fair. After all, each of them was entitled to half of everything and she wasn't going to squabble over who contributed what. She wanted this divorce to go through as quick as possible.

She signed the paper and picked up both cards. Number one on her list done.

Simone climbed back in her car and as she was pulling away, she saw Griffin enter the bank. A little too slow, Buddy.

Next, she drove to her lawyer's office and laid the photographs out on her desk. "I'd like to start divorce proceedings against my husband."

Anna Cotes looked at the pictures. "I guess there's no hope at reconciliation."

"None whatsoever."

"Do you think he will contest the divorce?"

"I doubt it. These pictures show he isn't interested in being married to me. I've already taken the furniture that I brought into the marriage and put it in storage. I went to the bank and removed half of the money in our joint account. I'm going to a real estate agent next to start selling the condo."

"Is his name on the condo title?"

"Yes."

"Then you can't list it unless both of you sign the real estate agreement."

Simone grimaced. She really hadn't wanted to speak with Griffin. She'd wanted others to do the negotiations between them.

"I will file a Notice of Family Claim in the B.C. Supreme Court and gather the other forms that you will need to sign. If you both agree to end the marriage then a separation agreement will establish the terms of the divorce. I will need the name of his lawyer."

"I don't know if he has one yet. I guess I can find out."

"Good. I'll draw the papers up and when they are ready I'll phone you to come in and sign them."

Simone left the office. She walked slowly to her car. As much as she hated to, she had to text Griffin and asked for his lawyer's name. She stopped in at a deli and bought a sandwich for her lunch then drove to her office.

* * *

Serena sat behind her desk adding up the previous day's proceeds. She was happy at how well her pub was doing. Business had been steadily increasing over the past year and she was thinking of starting to have theme nights for special days like Valentine's, St. Patrick's Day, and Hallowe'en.

Right now her staff was decorating the pub for Christmas. And they were given the choice of dressing up as elves for their shifts throughout December. She, herself, had a Mrs. Clause costume which she would start wearing the last week before Christmas.

Serena's phone pinged. It was a message from Jerry.

I can't continue seeing you because I can't marry anyone outside the Jewish faith. The only possible way for us to continue dating would be for you to convert to Judaism and I get the impression that you are against that.

"Marriage?" Serena said out loud in disbelief. "No one's been talking about marriage. We barely know each other."

She thought about texting that back to him then decided against it. Any relationship they might have had was obviously over before it even began. She would just let it go.

Serena remembered the piece of paper the mover, Doug, had given her at Simone's condo. She'd been texting a few men from the dating sites over the past month while waiting to see what happened between her and Jerry. They'd been more like two acquaintances meeting for lunch or drinks than dates and now that nothing was going to develop with him, apparently not even marriage, she was going to start meeting the other men.

The question was, did she want to try a date the old fashioned way, meeting up with Doug before knowing anything about him? At least by texting for a while she could weed him out if she wasn't interested. Going on a date first and then learning the man's history, his plans for the future, and his likes and dislikes second seemed backwards. But it had been done for centuries before technology and human kind had survived and thrived.

She thought about Doug. He was attractive and obviously single, well, hopefully single. She dug in her purse for his number and sent him a text using her burner. He answered immediately and they agreed to meet tomorrow evening at the Canadian Brewhouse and Grill. She didn't want him to know that she owned a pub just yet.

Serena finished her paperwork and made up a bank deposit. She walked out into the main room of the pub and smiled at the way it was being transformed. A large artificial tree with lights attached stood in one corner. Ethan, a bartender and one of the wait staff, was attaching large colourful balls to the limbs. Arleth and Noah, two more staff, were hanging decorations from the ceiling and Lenny was painting a winter scene on the front window.

Serena walked down the street to the bank, dropped her deposit bag in the chute, and returned to the pub. Before entering she stopped to admire the completed window scene. Since gnomes were popular he'd painted three of them, each with a tall red and green striped hat and a white beard. But instead of just the nose showing under the hat he'd added round, black eyes to each of their faces. One carried two gifts, another held a lantern, and the third had a Christmas tree. Serena smiled at the picture. The children would surely love it.

Serena entered the pub. Lunch customers had arrived and one of them had been delegated the task of helping Ethan run some garland. He was laughing as he held one end of the garland while Ethan pinned the other to the ceiling.

She smiled at the interchange. This was what she'd hoped for when she'd opened the pub. The customers considered this a relaxing, welcoming place to come to and she made sure she hired only pleasant and outgoing staff.

Serena headed back to her office. She wondered how her sister was doing and decided to send her a text.

How are you holding up?

She thought about telling Simone that Jerry had dumped her but figured it wasn't the time and certainly nothing compared to what Simone was going through right now.

Serena went into the kitchen to see how the new head chef was fitting in. When her former head chef had moved to Vancouver Island, she'd hired Jackson Harris to replace him. Jackson had graduated from culinary school two years ago and worked in a restaurant in Vancouver as a station chef then a junior chef before answering her ad. Until she owned a pub, Serena had no idea how many different kinds of chefs there could be in a kitchen. Only high-end, fancy restaurants had an executive chef. They didn't cook, just spent their time managing the kitchen staff, training, planning menus, and looking after the budget. In the smaller restaurants the head chef did all of that and, in some places, also cooked.

Since she did the menu and budget planning, she only needed one full-time and one part-time head chef. The head chef was in charge of the kitchen and oversaw the day-to-day activities. She also had two full-time and two part-time station chefs, one to cook the beef and pork and one to cook the chicken and fish each evening. She didn't have a junior chef but had kitchen porters to cut up the vegetables and grate the cheese.

Like most days, the kitchen was a flurry of activity. Everyone scurried around doing their job and getting the plates filled for the wait staff to deliver to the customers. Serena observed for a while then left. No one needed her input. Jackson seemed to have everything under control.

She watched the wait staff go from table to table taking orders and delivering food. Sometimes, when the pub was full she grabbed a pad and waited the tables or delivered plates. There was no way she was going to have customers grumble about having to wait for their orders to be taken or their food to arrive.

Back in her office she found a text from Simone.

Bank done, lawyer done, but can't do anything about selling the condo without Griffin's signature on papers and he hasn't gotten back to me with his lawyer's name.

Serena had never been married but knew love and attention and gentleness could quickly change to loathing and animosity and disgust in just a matter of days when it came to divorce. She'd seen that happen to some of her friends.

Need company?

I have an appointment but maybe after that.

Okay.

Even though she'd just received a shipment of bottled beer yesterday Serena took her order phone with its inventory software. Many of her customers had their favourite and she didn't want to run out, so she checked the stock every couple of days. She ordered from the large beer companies but also liked to stock local craft beer and cider. She first went to the back room and clicked on the codes on each of the boxes there then stayed out of Lenny's way while she physically counted the bottles and cans in the cooler.

She returned to her office and planned her next order. It was almost four o'clock when her phone pinged.

I can leave now. Let's meet at Mom's. I'll pick up the wine.

Serena sent a smiley face and grabbed her purse and jacket. It would be a slow drive to her mother's place in rush hour traffic.

Chapter Three

Simone slowed and waited for a gap in the oncoming traffic before turning into her mother's driveway. A high hedge blocked the rest of the front yard from Oak Street. Simone parked in front of the two car garage. The remainder of the back yard was taken up with a shed, a covered patio, and a flower garden where her mother spent much of her summer.

Simone climbed out of her car and looked at the dark house. Strange, she thought. No one had said Patricia and Lauren would be out this late. Then she shrugged. She knew very little of her mother's activities. She took the bag with its two bottles of wine from the trunk and walked to the back door. It opened before she could insert her key.

"I'm so glad you're here!"

"Mom? What's going on? Are you okay?" Simone stepped in and flipped the switch to light the entranceway. She took off her coat and hung it on one of the pegs along the wall.

"Yes, I'm fine. I'm waiting for Lauren to return." She followed Simone into the kitchen.

"Why in the dark?" Simone turned on the light.

"I never realized how peaceful the dark is. There's always been someone else in the house or the television set on. When Lauren left I found the quiet so relaxing that I never turned on anything."

"Where did Lauren go?" Simone looked around the u-shaped kitchen with its white cabinets, marble counters and backsplash, stainless steel appliances, and island with matching marble counter and four chairs. It was sparkling clean.

"I don't know. She took me to my line dancing after lunch and I went to my office when we returned. I heard the front door open and close a couple of times then Lauren came and told me she had to go out for a while in my car."

"Did she say where or for how long?"

"No. And it's strange. When she's gone out before, she's always been back to make dinner and eat with me."

"Have you tried phoning her?"

"Yes, and it just goes to voicemail. I've left three messages."

Simone opened the refrigerator door. There was a casserole dish and salad sitting on the middle shelf. "Well, she made something for dinner so she's expecting to come back. I wonder if she's had an accident."

"Oh, no." Patricia's hands flew to her face. Her eyes grew wide. "She could be injured in a hospital somewhere."

The back door opened and closed. Simone and Patricia exchanged glances.

"Lauren?" Simone mouthed.

Patricia shrugged.

They turned to see who walked in the kitchen.

Serena stopped in the doorway and looked from Simone to Patricia. "What's happening?"

"Lauren left this afternoon and hasn't come back." Simone took down three wine glasses from the cupboard. She opened one of the bottles and poured the wine.

Serena removed her coat and draped it over the back of one of the chairs at the island then sat down.

"She might have been in an accident," Patricia said taking two of the glasses and giving one of them to Serena. She sat beside her. "I've left her three messages on her cell."

"Have you phoned the hospitals?"

"I just got here a few minutes ago." Simone took a sip of her wine. "We've been discussing what to do."

"Has she done this before?" Serena asked.

"No, never," Patricia said. "She very seldom leaves at all and always tells me ahead of time. I was slightly surprised when she suddenly told me she was going out."

"I'll start dinner and then we will each phone a hospital." Simone turned on the oven then took the dish out of the fridge. She opened the oven door and placed it on a rack.

"What will we say?" Patricia asked.

"Just ask what room Lauren Huckley is in," Simone answered.

"And that will work?"

"I've done it when I want to visit a friend and didn't know what room they were in and I've been given it."

The three made their calls and none of the hospitals had a patient by that name.

"You said you heard the back door open and close a couple of times," Simone said. "Maybe we should check her room."

"Her room?" Serena looked at her. "What for?"

Simone shrugged. "I don't know. Her actions seem out of character. Maybe there's something there that will tell us why."

"Oh, I don't think we should be snooping through her things," Patricia protested.

"Let's just open the door and look in."

Simone didn't wait for an answer. She headed to the basement steps beside the entranceway and turned on the light. She went down, Serena and Patricia following.

"I really don't like this idea," Patricia said. "What if she comes home and catches us?"

"We'll hear her and just say that we were down here getting the Christmas decorations." Simone stopped outside

49

Lauren's door. She hesitated. They were invading a friend's privacy.

Simone tested the knob and it turned. She opened the door. The room was dark. She reached in and found the switch. The large room lit up. The bed in one corner was made, nothing was on top of the dresser, and all the drawers were closed. The closet doors were also closed. There was nothing to suggest someone lived there, no clothes on the bed, no books on the nightstand, no pictures anywhere. The room gave the impression of emptiness.

Simone tiptoed across to the closet and opened one of the doors. The hangers were bare. She opened the other. No clothes hung there and nothing was on the shelves above. There were no shoes on the floor.

Serena pulled open the dresser drawers. They, too, were empty.

"She's left?" Patricia sat on the bed in disbelief.

"It appears that way," Simone said. "And she stole your car to do it."

"Oh." Patricia seemed lost. "Why would she leave?"

"That, we have to find out," Serena said. She saw a piece of paper under the lamp on the night stand. She pulled it out and held it up. One word was printed on it in capital letters.

SORRY.

"Sorry?" Patricia asked. "What's she sorry for?"

"Let's go upstairs, have dinner, and discuss it." Simone went to the doorway and waited for the others to exit the room. She shut off the light, closed the door, and followed them upstairs.

"Do we want to eat in the dining room or in here?" Serena asked as she poured them each another glass of wine.

"Here is fine." Patricia took plates from the cupboard and cutlery from a drawer and placed them on the island.

Simone put the salad bowl and dressings on the counter then found the oven mitts and took the casserole from the oven. She set it on a hot pot trivet and they sat down to eat.

"So Lauren has packed up and snuck out of the house without saying she was quitting or even a goodbye." Serena dished up some of the macaroni and hamburger. "Just that one word, sorry, which means nothing. Is she sorry for leaving or for something else?"

Simone looked at her mother. "Did she give any indication that she was unhappy here, did you two have a fight?"

"No!" Patricia looked shocked. "We've always gotten along. We've had a lot of fun together. I thought she was happy here."

"Something happened to make her decide to leave," Serena continued. "What's changed in the past few days?"

"Nothing. We made plans to decorate the house and have friends over for a few drinks next week. The only difference in our lives is that Simone moved in."

Both Patricia and Serena looked at Simone.

"What?" Simone demanded. "I liked Lauren."

"Well, you must have said or done something to make her leave," Patricia accused.

"I didn't and how could you even think it? I had really liked her, giving her a cheque at Christmas as a thank you for her hard work and making sure I remembered her birthday. There is no way Lauren left because of me. I only saw her last night when we all had dinner together and this morning when she made me pancakes. And I thanked her both times for the meal."

"Then there must be some other reason," Serena said.

"I can't think of any," Patricia said. "I'm sure if there was an emergency with anyone in her family she would have told me. I'd have given her the time off."

"What would be another motive for her to leave?" Simone asked.

"I don't know," Patricia cried. "I don't know." She got up and left the table, her food barely touched.

"Maybe it's a good thing you moved in with her," Serena said. "At least she has someone here for her."

"Yes," Simone nodded. "I'll take tomorrow off and stay with her. Why do you think Lauren left? And don't say because of me."

"Maybe not you but maybe because you moved in."

"What's the difference?"

"Well, you're going to be here every day instead of just coming for a visit a couple of times a month. Maybe she was doing something, like counterfeiting or making moonshine on the side and she was afraid you'd find out."

"Really?" Simone raised her eyebrows. "That's the best you can do?"

"On such short notice, yes," Serena grinned.

"What if she is a criminal, though?" Simone said thoughtfully.

"But what would she steal from here? I'm sure we would have noticed if one of the paintings or sculptures Mom and Dad brought back from their travels disappeared."

"What if it wasn't something big? What if it was jewellery or money?"

"You mean like stealing from Mom's purse?"

"Or from her jewellery box or maybe even her bank account. I read an article about a caregiver who memorized the pin number of the man she was looking after and would borrow his card to withdraw some money for herself."

"Oh." Serena looked at her sister. "She used to take Dad shopping."

"Right. And she goes everywhere with Mom. She could have memorized Mom's pin and then remove the card from her wallet whenever she wanted money."

"I wonder what happened to Dad's card when he died. We better ask Mom."

"And we should check her jewellery and see her card."

The sisters left the kitchen and went through the dining room to the living room. It was a large room with a light grey, sectional sofa, two matching overstuffed chairs, a long coffee table, and end tables with lamps. There was a fireplace with two floor-to-ceiling windows on each side that overlooked the front yard. Through a doorway was the front entrance and the staircase to the upstairs. Patricia's office was straight down the hall from the door.

They stood in their mother's office doorway. The room hadn't changed from when they were young girls. The far wall and the one to the right were covered by floor to ceiling shelves filled with books. Patricia's large mahogany desk with two computers, a printer/copier, and a fax machine on it sat in the middle of the room and faced the windows in the left wall. There was a settee and two chairs around a small coffee table in front of the windows. Behind the door were two filing cabinets.

Patricia sat in the large swivel office chair behind her desk staring at her computer. They had never been allowed in their Mother's office all the years they were growing up. That had raised their curiosity and one day when their parents were gone they snuck into see what was so a secretive about it.

They scanned the shelves finding a mishmash of genres from mysteries, to sci-fi, to biographies. Many of them were signed by the author and some were addressed to Patricia Reed-Bell.

They found the novels written by their mother amongst the books on the shelves and snuck two of them out of the room. They read them under their covers in the safety of their bedrooms or sometimes together in one of their bedrooms. They exchanged the books when they were finished then discussed the story before replacing them and taking two more. It took them a year to read all their mother's books and they looked through the other books for another author to read.

Simone was sixteen and Serena fourteen when they discovered the books written by a woman named Angela Thompson. Their mother must have really liked her novels because she would write 'Mine' and sign her name on one of the inside pages.

Simone remembered being scandalized by the torrid, explicit love scenes in those books that made her blush. Serena had also been stunned at what their mother bought and read herself.

"Do Mom and Dad actually do things like that?" Serena had whispered after their first night of reading.

"I don't know," Simone had whispered back.

In spite of their shock, they'd read all the books their mother had and, as adults, they continued to buy each new Angela Thompson novel.

"Mom," Simone said from the doorway. They still didn't enter without invitation.

Patricia looked up and smiled wanly. "I'm sorry I got mad. It's just that this is all so sudden and hard to understand."

Simone exchanged looks with Serena. How to bring up the possibility that Lauren might be a thief? "Mom, did Lauren have access to your debit card?"

Patricia looked at them. "I'd occasionally give it to her when I didn't feel like going shopping."

"So she knows your pin number."

"Yes." Then she realized what Simone was asking. "Do you think Lauren stole some money when she had the card?"

"We'd have to go to the bank to find that out."

"Did you destroy Dad's debit card when he died?" Serena asked.

Patricia thought back. "I...I don't remember."

"When was the last time you checked your account? Do you have any bank statements?"

"I don't receive printed statements anymore. I don't bank on-line so if I want to check my deposits and withdrawals I have to go to the bank and get it printed out. I have better things to do."

"What about your jewellery?" Simone asked. "Has anything gone missing lately?"

"Not that I've noticed." Patricia shook her head. "But I don't wear as much jewellery as I used to."

"Can we take a look?"

"Sure." She stood up and the three went upstairs to Patricia's bedroom. It was large with a queen sized bed, two dressers, a walk-in closet, and an ensuite. Beside one of the dressers was a jewellery armoire with a full-length mirror.

Patricia went to the armoire and pulled open the door. Another mirror was at the top of the back wall and beneath it were slots full of various sized diamond, emerald, and pearl rings. Under that, were shelves with perfume and nail polish bottles. On the inside of the door were slats holding dangling gold and silver earrings and below them were hooks with matching necklaces.

"Is everything here?"

Patricia ran her fingers through the necklaces and earrings and then over the rings. "I think so."

"That's a relief." Serena sighed.

"You're wrong about Lauren. She wouldn't steal from me."

"We'll check your bank records tomorrow just to be sure," Simone said. "And we'll start looking for someone to replace Lauren."

Chapter Four

Serena sat at her table and sipped her morning coffee as she stared at the text from Simone.

Just leaving the bank. Someone has been using Dad's debit card to withdraw one thousand dollars four times a month since he died.

She quickly did the math. It had been twenty months since their father's death. Twenty times four was eighty thousand dollars. Someone had stolen eighty thousand dollars from their mother.

Unbelievable. Was it Lauren?

Don't know for sure but it is suspicious. I cancelled Dad's card and got a new one for Mom with a new pin number.

Good. Are you going to the police?

Yes, we are one our way there now.

Serena sent a thumbs-up emoji. She picked up her cup and left her condo. She lived on the third floor of the four storey building. While there was an elevator, she preferred to use the stairs. At the bottom she checked to make sure she had her keys then went out the door to the street. She turned left, went a few steps and opened the door to her pub.

The pub didn't open until ten o'clock and the room was quiet. She could hear voices and the clinking of pans in the kitchen as the staff prepared the day's menu. Serena walked to her office. She usually enjoyed this quiet time. But today it was spoiled by the news of the theft of her mother's money. She didn't know how much money her mother had or even how many accounts she had. Would the loss of the eighty thousand dollars have an effect on her finances?

When their father died, Patricia had given Simone Power of Attorney with Serena next in line if Simone was unable to carry out her duties. Both Serena and Simone were named Executors of her will. But, since their mother was capable of looking after herself and her finances, neither of them had asked any questions. After all, Patricia still did her own banking and shopping with the help of Lauren.

Maybe they shouldn't have been so trusting. Maybe they should have begun checking as soon as Lauren was hired. But there was nothing about her that had raised their suspicions. She seemed to have a genuine affection for Craig and Patricia, crying at Craig's funeral and vowing to stay with and take care of Patricia as long as she needed it.

Now she had disappeared and so had thousands of dollars of her mother's money.

Serena's burner phone pinged with a text from Doug.

I'm free for lunch if you are.

Serena thought about her plans for the day. Nothing out of the usual and there would be enough wait staff to handle the lunch crowd.

Perfect. Meet you at the Canadian Brewhouse and Grill at twelve.

Serena smiled for the first time that morning now that she had something to look forward to. She could hear her staff arriving to prepare for the lunch crowd which ran from ten until two and decided to go help with the preparations. It would take her mind off her mother and Lauren for a while.

Two hours later, Serena was pulling into the brewhouse parking lot. She had thought about changing from the usual jeans and sweater she wore to her office or when she helped in the kitchen, and putting on a more formal slacks and blouse but decided against it. Doug was a regular working man and she didn't have to dress up to go for lunch with him.

Serena walked into the brewhouse and looked around. It was half full and she spotted Doug in a far booth. She started towards him and realized when he stood to greet her that he had dressed for the occasion. Gone were the jeans and t-shirt. In their place were black slacks, navy blue sweater over a light blue shirt, and a black suit coat. His hair looked like he'd just come from his stylist. He gave her a hug and she smelled fresh aftershave. The man had made an effort to impress her.

Serena felt slightly underdressed next to him. She removed her black coat and hung it on the hook attached to the booth.

"Thank you for coming on such short notice," Doug said as they sat across from each other. "I guess I should have given you more time to change, though."

Serena felt her jaw drop. What the.... She thought about explaining why she hadn't changed then decided against it. She didn't owe this man anything. Besides, this was a brewhouse, not a fancy steakhouse, and they were having lunch, not dinner. If he wanted to dress up for it, that was on him.

The server came and set down menus. "Would you like something to drink?"

Serena ordered a coffee with cream and a glass of water. Doug asked for one of their house beers.

"My full name is Doug Lane. I am divorced with no children. My parents live here and I have one brother, two sisters, and no pets. You know what I do for work." He paused. "I can't think of anything else that would be on my profile if you had found me through a dating site."

"My name is Serena Bell. You met my sister when you moved her things. She is the only sibling I have. My father died almost two years ago and my mother lives on her own. I work in a pub in Richmond."

"I think you meant to say you own the B&B Pub in Richmond." Doug smiled.

Serena was shocked. He had checked up on her? It felt a little creepy but then everyone's information was out on the web. The only way you could avoid people learning about you was by not having a computer or cell phone.

"Yes, you're right. I do own the pub." She opened the menu and looked through the dishes.

"Is there a reason you didn't want to meet there?"

"I like to get away sometimes." Serena wasn't sure if she liked this man. He seemed to enjoy putting her on the spot. "How long have you been a mover?"

"I was a construction worker for fifteen years. My brother started the moving company two years ago and he needed some help, so last year I began driving truck all over the Greater Vancouver area picking up and dropping off people's possessions."

"That seems like hard work."

Doug shrugged. "It is."

The server came back with their drinks. She set Doug's beer in front of him then placed Serena's cup of coffee, a bowl of cream containers, and her glass of water in front of her. "Are you ready to order?"

"Yes," Doug said. "I'll have the prime rib with mashed potatoes."

The server looked at Serena.

"I'd like the Monte Crisco sandwich with fries."

The server nodded and left.

Doug tasted his beer and grimaced. "Not one of their better brews."

Serena took a sip of her coffee. It was good. No need to add cream or sugar. She preferred her coffee black but sometimes found the taste unpleasant and had to doctor it with cream and sugar in order to drink it.

The room began to fill with customers and the talking and laughter increased. Serena wondered how the lunch hour was going at her pub.

"So how do you happen to own a pub? It's not something you think of a woman doing. Did you get it in a divorce settlement?"

This time Serena prided herself in keeping her bottom jaw in place. Could this man sound any more sexist?

"I've never been married." She tried to keep her voice civil. "I bought a bar two years ago and revamped it into a pub."

Doug looked around the noisy room. "It must be a very lucrative."

"I do okay."

The server came over with their meal. Serena immediately started eating. She wanted to end this lunch date as quickly as possible.

"Have you always lived in Richmond?" Doug asked.

"No. I was raised in Vancouver."

"Even though you don't seem interested enough to ask, I'll tell you that I was born in Prince George and my family moved here when I was ten."

"Why?" Serena thought she should at least be polite and keep the conversation going. Nothing was worse than awkward silence.

"Why what?"

"Why did they move here?"

"My father is a professor and he applied for a position at UBC and was accepted."

"And your mother?"

"What about my mother?"

"What does she do?"

"She has spent her marriage making sure my father is happy."

Serena almost choked on a French fry. Had he really said that and with a straight face? Wait until she told her friends and Simone about this date. It sure would top any of their dating stories. She might even take the prize for meeting the most obnoxious man of the year.

They ate in silence. Serena tried to think of a neutral subject to talk about. "I like your sweater."

"Thank you. It's made from khullu, the official name of yak hair. It's soft like cashmere but more durable and warmer than cashmere."

Doug looked at her cream-coloured sweater. "I like your sweater also," he said without much enthusiasm.

"Thank you. It's camel."

"Camel?"

"Yes, because it's got two humps." Serena waited for the giggle or laugh she usually got from the statement.

Doug stared at her blankly and then snorted when he got the joke.

The server came over to pick up their plates. "Would you like the dessert menu?"

"Not for me," Serena said.

"Nor me."

"I'll be back with the bill."

Serena couldn't think of any other topic to talk about, so she pretended to be interested in the abstract painting on the wall. Let awkward silence reign.

"Do you like to travel?" Doug asked.

Apparently he didn't like silences.

"Yes." She'd read that this was one of the questions that could be asked on a first date. But she wasn't going to get drawn into discussing her favourite place to visit or where she wanted to go next. But she didn't have to worry.

"Me, too. I love going to Mexico and moving your sister was my first job since I got back from there last week. I'm actually looking at buying a condo in Puerto Vallarta and renting it out to tourists to make the payments. That way I can keep aside whatever weeks I want for me."

The server returned with the bill. Doug picked it up and looked at it. Serena was just about to thank him for lunch when he said.

"My share works out to thirty-three dollars; yours is twenty-six."

Serena nodded. It was fair. After all, was it sexist to expect the man to always pay for the meal? She took thirty dollars from her wallet and placed it on the table. Doug picked it up then paid for the full meal with a credit card.

Serena slid out of the booth and pulled on her jacket. "It was nice getting together," she said as politely as possible. "I have to get back to work." She hurried out of the brewhouse and to her car.

There was the old saying about promiscuous people putting a notch in their bedposts to mark each sexual partner they had bedded. Well, she had her own tradition. Since most of her meetings usually didn't end well and certainly didn't get as far as sex, she could only tell her bedpost about the date. For her bedpost would know if she tried lying about having had sex. This one was going to make a great story.

Her phone pinged.

We're decorating the tree. Want to come and help?

Just leaving Canadian Brewhouse and Grill. On my way.

She waved at Doug standing on the sidewalk as she drove away.

* * *

Simone and Patricia left the police station and climbed into Simone's car. Simone felt sorry for her mother. She was having a hard time absorbing the fact that Lauren had stolen so much money from her along with her car.

"I feel awful," Patricia said. "I never thought she would steal from us. You dad kept an eye on our accounts when he was alive and never found anything wrong after we hired her. I trusted her. I really trusted her. She was so caring and worked hard to look after your dad and then me."

"She's been doing it slowly and methodically." Simone sat without starting her car.

They had checked all of Patricia's accounts and investments and she was still very well off, having plenty of money, even if she never sold another book, to last her as long as she lived. But that wasn't the point. Lauren had committed elder financial abuse and needed to be caught and punished. Hopefully, the police would also be able to get some of Patricia's money back. It was in their hands and she was going to try and take her mother's mind off of it. After all, it was the Christmas season and time to set aside troubles for a while. But they had one more stop.

"Lauren has a key to your house, so we should get your locks changed."

"Oh, I didn't think about that."

Simone looked for the nearest locksmith on her cell phone then started the car and drove to the address. She went in and gave her mother's address to the receptionist.

"A locksmith will be there at nine Friday morning. Will someone be there to let her in?"

"Yes."

"Then you're booked."

"We have to be up and dressed early Friday morning," Simone told her mother when she was back in the car. "The locksmith will be there at nine."

"Good."

"Now, let's go home and decorate the house."

"Okay," Patricia nodded.

Simone pulled into the driveway and they entered the house. While Patricia made sandwiches, Simone sent Serena a text. Her sister replied she'd be right over. Simone went to the basement and hauled the boxes of her mother's decorations up to the living room, then her own that she had stashed with them. Was it only two days ago? She found the two pieces of the artificial tree each wrapped in a blue recycle bag and carried each piece up and laid them near the fireplace.

While they were eating lunch, Serena entered the house. "So tell me about what the police said." She took off her coat and sat beside them at the island.

"We gave them all the information we knew about Lauren, where she lived before moving in with Mom and Dad, when they hired her, where her parent's lived." Simone looked at Patricia. "We realized we knew very little about her. Did she have any hobbies, what she did on her day off, did she have friends, a boyfriend?"

"The constable said they would check with her family to see if they knew where she was," Patricia added. "It's not a high profile crime, so I don't think they will do much more than that."

Serena nodded.

"And a locksmith will be here on Friday morning to change the locks," Simone said. "I'll give you a new key when it's done."

"I'll put the dishes in the dishwasher if you two want to put the tree up." Patricia stood and gathered up the plates.

Simone and Serena went to the living room. Simone put a Christmas CD in the player on a credenza against the staircase wall while Serena removed the tree from the recycle bags. To the sound of *We Wish You a Merry Christmas,* they placed the bottom half of the tree in the stand and then set the upper section on top. Simone plugged in the lights to make sure they all worked. They carried it to the corner beside one of the tall windows. When Patricia joined them they talked and laughed about past Christmases as they added garland, different shaped and coloured balls, and family made decorations from when the girls were young.

"Do you remember making this in school?" Patricia showed Serena a red ball with small, plastic flowers, beads, and shells glued to it.

"Oh, yes." Serena took it in her hands. "The teacher provided the flowers and beads and then each of us was supposed to add something of our own. Those are the shells I gathered that summer we camped at Long Beach on Vancouver Island." She hung it on a tree branch.

"And this is one you made, Simone." Patricia handed her a gingerbread man made of cardboard and painted brown. It had small beads for eyes and buttons, and pieces of cloth for trim.

"Gosh, I sure was talented, wasn't I?" Simone laughed as she hung it up.

The CD finished and Serena put in another one. The first song was *Jingle Bells*. The sisters looked at each other and began to sing along. But they changed the words when they reached the chorus.

"*Single Bells, Single Bells,*
Single all the Way.
Oh what fun it is to be
Single every day."
They laughed when they finished.

"Gosh, I haven't thought of that in years," Serena said.

"Yeah. We used to sing that in our early twenties when we were both thought we would never find a husband."

"Well, that could still be my theme song."

"And it looks like it will be mine again." Simone felt a lump in her throat and she swiped at a tear in her eye. She took a deep breath. Now was not the time to break down over the ending of her marriage. "Let's get decorating the house."

She and Serena opened the boxes and dug through the decorations. It wasn't long before there was garland everywhere, hanging from the ceiling, trimming the windows, and woven in the banister to the upstairs. Round colourful wreaths of artificial branches, red holly berries, and plaid ribbon were hung on the outside of the front and back doors. A long wreath of gold branches and silver flowers was draped over the mantel of the fireplace. Lights trimmed the windows.

When they ran out of Patricia's decorations, Simone opened her boxes.

"I think we have enough," Patricia said.

"Oh, with Simone you can never have enough," Serena laughed.

"We've only just begun," Simone grinned. "We have the kitchen, the bathroom, and the dining room to do yet."

"Well, you two get at it and I'll pour the wine," Patricia said.

When the house was decorated to Simone's specifications the three women sat in the living room with their glasses of wine.

"Have you heard from Griffin?" Serena asked. "Is he going along with the divorce?"

"I sent him a text with my lawyers name, but I haven't heard back." She didn't say that she kept her phone shut off most of the time.

"Let's hope he doesn't cause any trouble."

"Hey, don't you have a date with Doug this evening?" Simone asked wanting to change the subject.

"No, that got pushed up to lunch today at the Canadian Brewhouse and Grill."

"So, that was why you were in Vancouver. How did it go?"

"Well," Serena grimaced. "His good looks are about the only thing he's got going for him."

"Oh, this sounds salacious." Patricia leaned forward. "Tell us all about it."

"Well, for one thing he knew I own a pub even though I only told him I work at one."

"Oh, that's disturbing." Simone shivered. "He checked up on you."

"That's what I thought but then it isn't hard to find out anything about anyone. It just bothered me."

"What else?" Patricia asked.

"His mom spent her life making his dad happy, I should have dressed up even though it was a lunch at a brewhouse, and owning a pub isn't really a woman's job."

"Sounds like you two are made for each other," Simone smiled. "Going on another date?"

"I really don't consider this was a date and I highly doubt it." Serena's phone pinged. She looked at it. "Well, a text from guess who."

"Oh, maybe his ears were ringing," Patricia grinned. "What does he say?"

"Hmmm," she read a little. "It seems to be a list of ways that I can improve myself."

"What?" Patricia gasped. "There's nothing wrong with you. I raised you, after all."

"Well, not according to him."

"What does he suggest?"

"My eyelashes are too short and I should get false ones. They will improve the appeal of my eyes immensely. I look a little pale, so should spend some time on a tanning bed. My wardrobe could use improvement and he listed some stores where I should shop. I should show more interest in my date. I didn't ask enough questions about him and his likes and dislikes. And I shouldn't try telling jokes."

"My god! What kind of a rock does he live under?" Simone asked. "Are there really still men who think like that?"

"Apparently. His last sentence is: I will contact you again just before Christmas. If you have made these improvements, then I will consider going out with you again, perhaps on New Year's Eve." Serena grinned at her mother and sister. "How lucky am I, another date with him."

"What joke did you tell him?" Simone asked.

"The one about the camel sweater."

"That is a funny one."

"He didn't think so."

Serena's phone pinged again. "Oh, great. He's now offering to step in and run my pub for me. Since owning and operating a pub isn't really a woman's job, he's willing to quit his job and take it over for me."

"Is he joking?" Simone couldn't believe she'd just heard that.

"Nope. He'll come by sometime this week, so I can walk him through how to run it. His exact words are: 'It takes a man's business-oriented mind to make a success of any venture. A woman doesn't have that type of thinking'."

The three women stared at each other.

"I feel I'm being tricked, maybe even punked by him," Serena said. "He really can't still think this way."

"Are you going to answer him?" Patricia asked.

"I don't think it's worth my time."

"If you don't, he might show up at your pub."

"Yes, he might take a no answer as a yes," Simone agreed. "After all, he's probably thinking no woman could turn down such an offer, especially put in such a delicate, selfless way. In his mind, he's doing you such a big favour."

Serena spoke out loud as she typed. "I am not going to change who I am for you or any other man. You just aren't that important to me. And my pub has been a success for the past year and it will continue to be without you."

"Good." Patricia clapped her hands.

"And on that note, I should get back to my pub." Serena stood.

"Before you go," Patricia said. "Tomorrow is Thursday. Time for my visit to the Arbutus Hall Retirement Home to play backgammon and have tea with my friends. Lauren always took me. Would you girls like to come with me instead?"

"I can take you." Simone looked questioningly at Serena.

"I'll come here and we can all go together," Serena said.

"I'm usually there from two to four."

"I'll be here at one-thirty."

Chapter Five

Serena climbed out of the front passenger seat then helped her mother out of the back. Patricia was dressed in a cream, sleeveless jumpsuit with a blue jacket. She had a blue, burgundy, and cream scarf tied in a large bow at her neck. The burgundy in the scarf matched her burgundy shoes and purse. She wore a tan, cashmere wrap against the cold. A bit overdressed to play cards, Serena thought.

The three of them strolled over to the double door and Simone opened one. She followed the other two into the foyer. There was an office to the right and a bench to the left.

"Come with me," Patricia said, setting off down a hallway.

They came to an open door to the left and entered a large common room. There was a pool table, square tables with four chairs, two sofas, three arm chairs, and a narrow table against the wall with a coffee urn, cups, juices boxes, and individually wrapped cookies and muffins. In the corner was an upright piano. The room was decorated for Christmas and holiday music softly played.

Two men and one woman stood around the pool table, cues in their hands while they watched a second woman make a shot. A woman was putting together a puzzle on one of the square tables, and two couples were playing bridge at another. Two women sat on the sofa and one in a chair. Everyone in the room was smartly dressed, with the ladies' hair perfectly styled and the men's hair trimmed short.

"Patricia, come sit with me," one of the women called.

"Mona." Patricia walked over and sat beside the elderly woman.

"And who are these two young ladies?" Mona looked up expectantly.

"These are my daughters, Simone and Serena. Girls my friends Mona, Cora, and Adele."

"Nice to meet you, Simone and Serena," the three ladies said.

"Where is Lauren today?" Mona asked.

"Um, she couldn't make it."

They had discussed what Patricia would say to that question and decided on a simple answer. Serena was glad that the other women accepted it.

A handsome older man dressed in gray slacks and beige shirt walked into the room. He wore wire-rimmed glasses and his gray hair was combed to the side. "Ah, you came."

He strolled over to where Patricia had stood, put his hands on her shoulders, and kissed her cheek.

"Bert, I'd like you to meet my daughters, Simone and Serena." She turned to them. "Girls, this is Bert Madden."

Bert held out his hand and each woman shook it. "I'm so pleased to finally meet you. Patricia has been proudly telling me about you two for months. Simone owns a literary agency and Serena owns a pub. Both of you are highly successful women."

Well, this is he first time we've heard about you, Serena thought but didn't say. She liked this older man who had the manners of a by-gone era.

"We have a very good role model," Simone said.

"Are you ready, my dear?" Bert smiled and held out his arm to Patricia.

"I am." She slipped her hand in the crook of his elbow. They started in the direction from which Bert had come.

"Where are you going?" Serena asked.

Patricia winked. "He's going to show me his etchings."

"He draws? That's wonderful." Serena thought of the process of using strong acid to cut into parts of a metal surface that wasn't protected by wax, to create a design. It was beautiful work. "Do you have a workshop here? Can we see them?"

"Oh, you poor girls," Mona said.

"What?" Simone asked as they watched their mother and Bert leave the room.

"Back in our day when a man asked a woman if she wanted to go to his apartment to see his etchings, it meant a dalliance."

"A what?" Serena asked then felt herself blushing. "Oh."

"They're not!" Simone protested.

"Oh, but they are," Mona said with a knowing smile.

Serena looked at Simone. Their mother did write romance novels and she read the spicy novels written by Angela Thompson but that didn't mean she actually had sex at her age, did it?

"Why do they call it seeing his etchings?" Simone asked.

"Sit down and I'll tell you." Mona patted the sofa.

Simone sat down beside her and Serena sat on a chair.

"You've heard of the movie producer, Alfred Hitchcock, I presume," Mona began.

"Yes." Both sisters nodded.

"His very first sound movie was *Blackmail* and it came out in 1929. In it, the male lead would use the line to get women into his townhouse, so he could seduce them. Later on, in the 1933 movie *She Done Him Wrong*, Mae West said, "Why don't you come up sometime and see me," which basically meant the same thing. It has since been shortened to 'Come up and see me sometime.' In our time everyone knew what they meant."

"Well, I've never heard of either of them," Serena said.

"That's because our language has lost its eloquence," Adele said with disgust. "It's been degraded almost to the grunts and one or two word phrases of the cave people. And the f-word is its most frequently used word. People can't talk without peppering their sentences with that word. It's almost as if they can't think of real words anymore."

"Right," Cora agreed. "We've communicated through the use of our language and the fact that we can write it down for others to read. Now, it's been reduced to the small words and short phrases that a preschool child uses. And, once we lose that ability to speak or write words that describe life around us and our experiences, we lose our ability to see and understand things."

"Were you ladies teachers?" Serena asked.

"How could you tell?" Cora smiled.

"I had an English teacher who decried the loss of the refinement and classiness of the words used in the 1700 and 1800s. She said that the words from those centuries are considered old-fashioned and out-dated now."

"And enough of our English lesson today," Mona said, briskly. "Who wants to play *Dirty Black Bitch*?"

"What?" Serena was surprised at the quick change of topic and of her choice of words.

"Also known as the card game *Hearts*." Mona smiled sweetly.

"Oh, we know how to play that," Simone said. "Why do you call it *Dirty Black Bitch*?"

"Because no one wants to get stuck with the Queen of Spades."

"We could also play *Stab Your Grandmother* or *Shithead*," Adele grinned.

"Card games, too?" Serena gulped. These were not your typical charming little, old ladies.

"Yes," Mona nodded.

"I think we'll play *Hearts*," Simone said.

"Okay," Mona nodded. "We'll teach you the other games next time you come."

"I have to go to my room and lie down," Cora said standing. "But you ladies have fun."

Mona went to a shelf and got a deck of cards and met the other three women at a table. She shuffled the cards and then began dealing cards face up. "First jack deals," she said.

The first jack landed in front of Serena. She gathered up the cards and added them back to the deck and shuffled. She dealt the full deck, so each player had thirteen cards. She looked at her hand. The object of the game was to have the lowest score when someone reached one hundred and that was done by not taking any tricks that included the Queen of Spades or any hearts, since they were the ones that counted against each player.

Serena had a mix of all four suits with the highest card being the king of clubs. It was a fairly good hand for not taking a trick, but she had to pass three cards to Adele on her left and receive three cards from Simone on her right. That could screw up her whole hand. She had four small spades and decided to keep them in case she received the queen or any high spade. Since there was no trump she decided to get rid of the king, nine, and seven of clubs. The lower the cards she kept the less likely she was to take a trick.

She passed her cards and picked up the ones from Simone: ace, jack and ten of diamonds. She put them with her other two diamonds and waited for play to begin.

By the time Patricia and Bert returned to the common room an hour later, Mona had won two games and Adele one. Serena was surprised at how focused the two women had been on the games, making quick and decisive plays. They must play a lot.

"Your mother and I just had some wine but would you like some refreshments?" Bert asked Serena and Simone.

Serena was amazed at how nonchalant he was after just having had sex their mother. "I need to get back to my pub."

"And I have a manuscript I have to finish editing," Simone added.

"Well, I guess that means we're leaving," Patricia smiled. "Bye Mona and Adele."

Bert bent and kissed Patricia on the cheek. "See you again soon."

* * *

"Really, Mom? You come here for sex?" Simone started the car and drove out of the parking lot.

"No, I come here for the company and the pool games and the tea. The sex is just a bonus."

"Well, I didn't see you play any games," Serena said.

"That's because you two had to leave. Usually Lauren drops me off and picks me up when I send her a text." She paused. "Well, she used to."

Simone glanced at Serena. There was much they didn't know about their mother.

"I don't know why you two are surprised. After all, you know what I write. Not everything in my novels is made up. Some, I write from experience."

"Are you saying you were doing research for a novel today?" Serena asked winking at Simone.

"Maybe," Patricia smiled.

"So you get together with Bert for sex?"

"No, we get together for companionship. We talk, we hold hands and go for walks, we make love. He's actually pretty good in bed."

"Mom!" Simone exclaimed.

"Eww!" Serena cried.

"What? Sex is only for the young? People don't think of seniors as being vibrant or having a sex life. Did you know that there is a retirement home in Sweden that provides a sex positive environment? They have what they call a pleasure basket filled with sex toys, creams, and a Do Not Disturb sign. Residents can purchase any of the items and it helps them continue or rediscover a healthy sex life."

"So the seniors go bed hopping at night?" Serena asked.

"It's not always about sex. It's about closeness, and intimacy, and hugs. I've been very lonely since your father died. I began visiting a friend at the home and met Bert. He is such a sweet, caring man."

Serena heard the wistfulness in her mother's voice and wanted to take her in her arms. She realized that Patricia was a lucky woman who had found a great man to marry and then had forty wonderful years with him. And just because he died, it didn't mean that she had to stop living herself or for that matter, stop having sex, something she obviously enjoyed.

Simone slowed and pulled into the driveway.

"Come in, Serena," Patricia said. "I have something I want to show both of you."

Simone and Serena followed their mother into her office. She sat down behind her desk and opened the bottom drawer on the right. She pulled out a folder and set it on her desk.

"I know you two used to come in here and sneak the novels I wrote to read in your bedrooms."

"How could you?" Simone sputtered. "We were careful. We hid them under our mattresses and only took them out to read after going to bed so you wouldn't stumble in on us."

"And we made sure you weren't home when we removed them and when we returned them," Serena added.

"You two wouldn't make good criminals. You left the gaping hole where they were on the shelf."

Simone and Serena looked at each other and laughed. "We had to know where they belonged," Serena said.

"And here I thought we were being so smart," Simone added. "So you knew we also read the books written by Angela Thompson. Those were pretty hot."

Patricia opened the folder and turned it towards her daughters. They leaned over and read the contract between a publisher and Angela Thompson. Under her name was the legal name of the writer: Patricia Reed-Bell.

"You're Angela Thompson?" Simone stared at her mother. She thought of the intense, explicit, sex scenes in the Thompson books. Her mother had written them. And in her words, she'd researched them.

Hopefully, they had all been with their father and not lovers like her characters.

"I've enjoyed my writing career, my whole life, in fact. Marriage to your father was the best but it's time for me to get on with the next chapter of my life. Because, as long as I'm alive, I'm going to be living. And that might be with Bert."

As Patricia returned the folder to the drawer, Simone noticed that she had moved her wedding and engagement rings from her left hand to her right.

Chapter Six

Just after lunch on Friday Simone hit the 'Send' button on her computer and sat back with a sigh. Another manuscript had successfully gone through the first round of editing and was now sent back to the author to agree or disagree with the changes. She and the writer could go through many rounds of edits on the manuscript before it was ready to send out to publishers. Sometimes, she'd receive a manuscript that had a nearly perfect flow to its storyline and needed little work. Those ones she really liked.

Simone looked around her office. She loved her job. It was so exciting to sift through the hundreds of emails, each with a synopsis and first three chapters attached, that her agency received each month. And it was enjoyable to find the right story idea and decide what publishers might be interested in it. An email would be sent to the writer requesting the remainder of the manuscript. If it fulfilled the promise of the first three chapters then a contract was sent to the writer. Once signed the editing began.

Then came the pitch the publishing houses and ultimately the email back from a publisher who wanted to publish it. More contracts were signed, cover design decided, and sometimes more edits made before the publisher thought it was right. After that it could be eighteen months to two years before the actual book came out. So for the writer it could be three years from the time they send out their first queries to when they have the book in hand.

The only down side to the business was having to tell a writer that their manuscript wasn't what she were looking for right now. For, contrary to other literary agencies, she thought the writer should be told even if it was a form email. The writer had put a lot of time and effort, in some cases years, into writing thousands of words of their story and they should be treated with a little respect.

But many writers were unwilling to wait the three years to have their book published. They decided to go the self-publishing route, usually through Amazon or with a vanity press that took the writer's money and gave them books to sell on their own. There were also hybrid publishers who charged for their services but also helped the writer market and sell their books.

For writers who wanted to self-publish or go through a vanity press, her agency offered services as an editor because professional editing was what separated the good books from the bad. No reader wanted to pay money for a book that had spelling mistakes, plot irregularities, and characters whose hair colour or name changed half way through the book.

Simone looked at the clock. She wondered how Serena and her mother were doing. After the locksmith had changed the locks, Simone had taken Patricia to Serena's pub. Patricia had insisted that she could look after herself but Simone and Serena had quietly discussed the situation and decided it was best to have someone with their mother at all times. Although Lauren had seemed like a nice, caring person, she had stolen from Patricia. And now that they had cut off her money supply, both in her job and Patricia's bank account, they really didn't trust that she wouldn't come back and maybe rob her of her jewellery. They just didn't feel their mother was safe.

Simone took out her phone. *How are things going?*

First, Mom filled all the salt and pepper shakers on the tables, then she wiped the shelves under the counter. That took longer than it should have--I think she was flirting with Lenny. Now she's sitting at a table with her laptop.

Simone smiled. Serena had been worried about how to keep their mother occupied. Apparently, Patricia had found her own ways to spend her time.

Simone's phone pinged. A text from Griffin.

I've been trying to phone you. To save money and because we both want this divorce to go through as quickly and smoothly as possible I think we should use the same lawyer. I already phoned Anna Cotes and asked if that would be okay with her. She said as long as you agreed and we both understood that if there was a conflict we would each have to find another lawyer, then it was fine with her. What do you think? We have an appointment at ten on Monday afternoon. When the separation papers are signed we can find a real estate agent.

Simone stared at the text. After the initial first couple of days where he'd sent her many texts and left phone messages, he'd been silent. She'd been afraid he was going to fight her, although she couldn't think why. Now she was relieved.

How her life had changed. And even though she'd suspected he was seeing someone and had been given the proof, it somehow seemed surreal that they were now discussing their divorce in a strangely calm way. It was almost as if they were discussing where to go on vacation.

But he was right. It would be cheaper and easier if they used the same lawyer. There would be no worries about paperwork not being sent or received, it would all be in the same office.

Yes, it is okay with me. Simone sent back.

See you Monday.

Simone brought up Serena's number. *It looks like Griffin is agreeing to everything.* Simone sent. *We're even using the same lawyer.*

If things are going that well, we'd better get you on some match making sites.

What? Are you serious?

Hey, it's Christmas. You can't spend it alone.

I have you and Mom.

That's not the same. Besides, Mom has Bert and I'm still looking for the right man. I'll help set you up on a couple of the sites when I bring Mom back tonight.

Simone sighed. She understood what her sister was doing but the last thing she needed was to jump into another relationship, especially so soon after finding out her marriage was ending. But she knew that once Serena got an idea in her mind there was no stopping her. It was best to go along with it. Besides, just because she was on the sites didn't mean she had to go on any dates. If she wanted to get out of the house for a while she could meet her friends.

I'll pick up something for dinner. Simone sent back. *Remember, we also have an interview with Ellie Fendley as a prospective caregiver for mom this evening.*

Serena sent back a thumbs up emoji.

Simone spent the rest of the afternoon discussing the synopsis and first chapters of three manuscripts with her agents. They went over the pros and cons of the subject matter of the stories and discussed what publishers might be interested in them. They finally decided to ask for the remaining chapters of two of the manuscripts.

Just before leaving her office, Simone phoned a restaurant she liked and ordered the three meat plate, a Caesar salad, mashed potatoes, sweet corn, gravy, and buns to be picked up at five o'clock. She stopped in, paid for the food, and took the paper bags home. She'd just set them on the counter when Serena and Patricia walked in.

"How was your day?" Simone asked her mother.

"It was fun. That bartender sure is handsome." She grinned at Serena. "You should be dating him."

"I told you I don't believe in workplace romances. And because I own a pub and not a bar, I prefer that Lenny is called a beverage server."

"Sit down." Simone decided not to get fancy by placing the food in bowls. She set the boxes on the island and added plates and cutlery. "Did you get any writing done, Mom?"

"Oh, yes," Patricia said as she filled her plate. "I've heard of authors who do much of their writing in a restaurant or coffee shop and I always thought it would be hard to concentrate with all the noise around them. But it is kind of comforting to be in the crowd. Plus, I sure did hear a lot of different conversations. It's amazing what people talk about in public."

"Have you heard anything from the police?" Serena asked. She poured gravy on her potatoes.

"No." Simone shook her head. "I'll give them a week and then call."

"When is Ellie Fendley coming?" Serena asked.

"At seven."

They had looked through many business websites advertising caregivers for seniors. All offered twenty-four/seven support, full homecare services from cooking to exercise, and companionship and whatever the client needed. But since both she and Serena had their own businesses they'd also checked out Carer.ca, a service that connected independent caregivers and companions with those who needed them. They had read many profiles and had contacted three who had sounded promising.

When they were finished eating Simone and Serena cleaned off the island while Patricia took her laptop to her office. The front doorbell rang. Simone hurried to answer it.

"Hello. I'm Ellie Fendley from Carer.ca. We spoke on the phone." The woman in her late twenties smiled at Simone. She was tall and heavy set and her curly, brown hair was cut short. She had a brown envelope in one hand.

"I'm Simone Bell." She'd begun introducing herself by maiden name again. "Come in."

Simone led Ellie to the living room where she introduced Serena and Patricia.

"As you know we are looking for a caregiver for our Mother," Simone began after they'd sat down. "We want someone to come in three days a week and if that works out eventually move in permanently."

She and Serena had decided Simone would stay in the house with their mother until they had found someone they could trust.

Ellie nodded. "I do look after another woman two days a week, so three days here would be perfect for me." She handed over the brown envelope. "These are the letters of reference I told you about and a list of my services."

Simone opened the envelope and took out the sheets of paper. As she read each one she handed it to Serena who then passed it on to Patricia. They laid out how many months or years Ellie had worked for the families and the reason for her leaving. She left two because the family member had moved into a seniors' home and the third was because the person had died. All of them had glowing comments about Ellie's gentle, compassionate nature and her ability to provide all the care needed. At the bottom were phone numbers if Simone wanted to contact the writers of the letters.

"May I keep them?" Simone asked.

"Oh, yes. They are copies. I keep the originals."

"And you charge twenty-two dollars an hour."

"Yes, but we can discuss a daily or even a weekly rate."

"Mom, Serena, do you have any questions?"

"What type of vehicle do you drive?" Patricia asked. "And how much accident insurance do you have?"

"I have a Grand Cherokee and a firm stool I set down for those who need help up into the seat. I have five million dollars insurance."

"If we wanted you to move in, how would that work with the other woman you look after?" Serena asked.

"I have a fellow worker who is willing to take over her care."

"Thank you for coming," Simone stood. "We will discuss this and get back to you."

"I look forward to hearing from you," Ellie said as she went out the door.

"What do you think?" Simone asked when she was back in the living room.

Serena held up the paper with Ellie's list of chores. "She seems willing to do almost anything: laundry, errands, appointments, meals, bathing, whole house cleaning, exercises, and walking, and taking client to theatres, movies, and out for other entertainment. What about you, Mom?"

"We still have two more to interview, but she does sound promising," Patricia said.

"Good." Serena turned to Simone. "Now where is your computer? It's time to find you a boyfriend."

Simone held back a sigh. If she wanted to have a peaceful Christmas, she knew she had to agree to sign up on a dating site. She went upstairs and brought down her laptop.

"Hey, Mom. Do you want to sign up, too?" Serena asked.

"No, Dear. I found my man the old fashioned way." She smiled and went to her office.

Simone raised her eyebrows at Serena. "It sounds like she's serious about Bert Madden. Maybe we should find out more about him other than that he's good in bed."

"Yes. What did he work at? Was he married? How much money does he have?"

"I'll talk with Detective Raymond Webster tomorrow and see what he can dig up."

Serena nodded.

Simone carried her laptop to the dining room table and opened it. "I'm not even sure if I want to start seeing men so soon after my break-up, and so close to Christmas. Besides, I heard some people don't like the men or women they find on these sites. Jilly, one of my editors, says she put in a lot of time and effort and never did find the right guy. She got a lot of sexy messages, though, and she had to block some of the guys' phone numbers."

"Don't be so negative." Serena sat in front of the computer. "You have to take your mind off your divorce and you can do that by celebrating the holidays by dating some new men. And I'm going to be too busy finding my own dates to go out with you. And so is Mom. In fact, she's way ahead of us."

"Okay, then I'll look at having a situationship, not anything serious."

"Situationship? What type of dating is that?"

"It's informal dating."

"With maybe a little sex thrown in?" Serena grinned.

Simone laughed and nudged Serena with her elbow.

Serena brought up a dating site on the computer and together they created Simone's profile giving her age-thirty eight, gender, and general appearance-medium height, normal weight, blondish hair. Simone uploaded a photo to the site, listed her hobbies, and what she was looking for in a man. She thought about saying 'straight' but decided against it. She doubted any of the men who wanted to connect with a woman on this site were gay.

"Just to give you a little warning," Serena said as she typed. "I've been stood up, I've met guys who are looking for a free ride, and I've met men who were only looking to hook-up for sex. Many of those even admitted they were married and just wanted a little excitement in their lives."

"Great."

"Don't get me wrong. There are a lot of nice men out there who, like you and me, are looking to form a long-term relationship with someone. However, you might want to get a burner phone. Many people, especially women, use them on these dating apps."

"Why?"

"Some people don't like giving out their primary phone number to a stranger. They don't like that the person has their number if the dating doesn't work out. I have one."

"But can't you block that number, like Jilly did?"

"Yes, but the person could phone using a different number."

"This is sounding less and less appealing."

"I'm just giving you a heads up on some things to watch for."

"I'll wait and see if I have any interest before I buy a burner."

Serena went into one of the dating sites where she was a member and showed Simone some of the men who the site thought she might be interested in.

"This is known as the dog guy." She pointed to a man who was kneeling beside a golden retriever. "There is that saying that animals and babies can recognize nice, caring people and these guys think showing a picture with a cat or dog makes them look like a sweet, trustworthy person."

Serena looked through a few more pictures and pointed to another. "He's the FWB guy."

"FWB?" Simone had seen those letters before but couldn't remember their significance.

"Friends With Benefits. He's a lot like the guy who says he's here for a good time, not a long time." Serena looked at Simone. "They might be for you since you only want a situationship for now."

Simone grimaced. "This is getting too complicated. I met Lucas in the supermarket and Griffin through friends. That seems so much easier than all this."

"Come on, older sister, get with the times. With over eight thousand dating websites all over the world it's quite common for people to sign up for at least one. Thirty-six percent of Canadians have used a site or app and eighteen percent have tried online dating."

"That's not a very high percentage."

"That's true, but it shows that many people are looking for a partner on them."

Chapter Seven

After saying goodbye to Serena, Simone typed 'online dating' into her browser and clicked on the magnifying glass. *About 2,790,000,000 results (0.45 seconds)* showed up at the top of the page. She stared at the number. How could there be so many sites? How could a person read them all?

She scrolled down the first page. There were different dating sites listed, a *Police Warn About Online Dating* section, and below that *People Also Ask* with some questions and answers about dating sites.

She found *The Best Dating Sites for Introverts, Apps and Websites for Over 50, The Ugly Truth About Online Dating,* and *Top Ten Best Dating Sites and Apps in Vancouver.* There was even some that offered subjects for conversation starters on your first date. My goodness, how did a person choose?

Simone clicked on one and began reading that a person should talk with a potential mate for three weeks online before switching to in person. That way your expectations will still be open and you can see if they embellished on their profile. And you will know enough about them that you will be more relaxed in their company.

Three weeks sounded good to her since she really wasn't interested in meeting anyone right now anyway. She would point that out to Serena and that should keep her sister from pressuring her into actually going out with someone.

She read a few more sites. One of them warned women that while there were some men who actually did want a permanent relationship, there were those who were just looking for sex. They figured that women on these sites were willing to sleep with any man they agreed to meet. The site further cautioned that women could possibly receive suggestive messages, pictures of the men's private parts, or outright propositions for sex.

One had a list of don'ts for women, like never give your phone number or email, always show up at the first meeting rather than have him pick you up, so he doesn't know where you live, and never leave your drink alone.

The last two made her almost afraid to meet up with any man who contacted her. How could she tell the good from the bad?

Simone thought about sending a message to Raymond Webster about running a check on Bert Madden, then she decided it might be better to find out a little more about Bert than his name and address.

She closed her computer and walked to her mother's office. Patricia was sitting on the settee reading a book. She looked up when Simone knocked.

"Come in, Dear."

Simone sat in one of the chairs opposite her.

"All set up on your dating site?"

"Apparently so. Now all I've got to do wait for the men to come flocking to my profile." She decided not to tell her mother about the warnings for women she'd read. "Can we talk about Bert?"

Patricia set down her book. "What do you want to know?"

"It seems you have been visiting him for a while. Why haven't you told us about him before?"

Patricia smiled. "Did you tell me about every boy you went out with when you were young or every man you were seeing before marrying Lucas or after he died?"

"Well, no. But that's different."

"How?"

Simone wasn't sure how to answer that. "We had no money to worry about."

"So you think he's after my money?" Patricia raised one eyebrow. "That it isn't me he wants to spend time with?"

"No, that's not what I'm saying." This wasn't going the way she'd wanted. "It's just that some men want a free ride."

Patricia laughed out loud. "Do you know what it costs to live in that place? Fifty-five hundred dollars a month. I think he has his own money."

Simone was surprised at the figure. Then another thought hit her. What if he was running out of money at that price? Finding a rich woman like her mother would take away his money worries. But she would leave that up to Raymond to find out.

"How long has he lived at Arbutus Hall?"

"Two years. He tried living alone but didn't like it. He enjoys having friends close to do things with. Plus, he likes that his meals are cooked for him and someone comes in to clean once a week. He got tired of eating takeout pizza or heating up garlic ribs and fries."

Typical man. But why was he interested in her mother? He already was being looked after by the staff. Ahhh, maybe he needed a beddie, someone to scratch his itch.

* * *

It was just after nine when Serena drove through the pub's full parking lot and parked behind the building in the spot reserved for her condo. She walked back to the street and into the pub. She smiled. There was a hockey game on the big screens and the room was full of Vancouver Canuck fans. She liked that parents brought their children to eat and watch the game together. She enjoyed seeing the high fives and fun rivalry among the customers at each table and sometimes between the tables.

Serena went into the kitchen to see if they needed any help.

"No, we're handling it okay," Jackson said as he dished up a bowl of chili.

She nodded and headed to the counter. Lenny was busy opening six bottles of beer and there was a list of drink orders waiting to be filled. She grabbed three mugs and pulled on the draught beer tap and filled them, opened one cider bottle, and scooped the ice from the bin into two glasses and sprayed ginger ale into them from the pop gun. The server set them on a tray and headed to a booth with four adults and two teenagers.

She then took two beer bottles from the cooler behind her, opened them and set them on the counter. She reached up and took down two wine glasses. She poured red wine into both of them and placed them beside the beers.

It was times like this that she missed being able to do some fancy bartending moves. She'd like doing flips with the bottles, palm spins of the glasses, and swoop pour cuts. It was fun to see the surprise on the customers' faces at the bar as they watched theirs or someone else's drinks being prepared.

"Good evening, Serena."

Serena put a smile on her face as she turned towards the man with wavy black hair, facial stubble, and blue eyes. He wore a white shirt under a black leather jacket. He hadn't changed a bit since she'd last seen him in the summer. "Hello, Darren. What are you doing here?"

"What? Can't a guy come and see his former girlfriend?"

Serena sighed. "We have nothing to say to each other."

"Why are you being so hard to get along with? You know we had a good thing going last summer. Why can't we just start over again?"

"Because there were just too many of us in that relationship. I don't need to go through that again." Serena wiped the counter with a damp rag.

"Hey, I've changed. I'm a one-woman man now. And you're the woman I want."

"Well, that's not how it works. My motto is not to be pricked twice by the same prick."

Darren grabbed his chest. "Oh, that's harsh. What happened to forgiving people who make mistakes?"

"I don't give second chances. If you didn't respect me enough to be faithful the first time around, you won't the next time either."

"I'll give you a while to think about it."

"Do you want something to eat or drink?" she asked.

Serena had no time to get into a discussion with him. He liked to put a person on the spot and make their statements sound stupid. She still couldn't believe that she had thought she was in love with him, that she had even hoped they might get married. They'd met on a dating site and came together over their mutual love of motorcycles. They spent last spring and summer touring around the lower mainland and on Vancouver Island.

It was when she'd been watching a B.C. Lions football game on television at the pub and saw him on the Jumbotron with not one but two women that their relationship had ended. For when they noticed themselves on the big screen, he'd kissed each of the women long and hard, ruling out them being his sisters.

"Yeah, I'll have chicken wings and you know what I like to drink."

"Go find a table and one of the servers will bring them to you."

"Why don't you bring them and we can talk further?"

"There's nothing more to say. We're not getting back together."

"We'll see." He winked at her and walked to a small table in a corner.

"I thought you were through with him." Lenny came and stood beside her.

"I am. But he wants to get back together."

"If he gives you any trouble, let me know."

Serena smiled. Lenny had worked for her ever since she opened the pub and they had become friends. He was single and having as much trouble finding a permanent relationship as she. They'd spent many a night commiserating with each other over a break-up and at their lack of a love life as they cleaned up after closing.

"I don't think I have to worry about him," she said.

Serena put Darren's order in for the chefs and continued serving up drinks. When the wings were ready she handed the plate and bottle of Strombo ale to Noah and pointed to Darren. He'd been watching because he smiled and waved at her. She ignored him.

After the pub shut down and the clean-up was done, Serena climbed the stairs to her condo. Getting a place above her business had been the best move she'd made other than opening the pub. Being so close to her work meant she didn't have to get up too early, she didn't have to contend with traffic, and when the long day was over, she was home in a matter of minutes.

The condo was a one bedroom with den. It had a large kitchen, dining room, and living room. The bathroom was small but then she didn't spend too much time in it. There was a deck off the living room with a view over a park. She could watch couples walk hand in hand, families having picnics, and kids playing games. And the neighbourhood was quiet. It would be the perfect life if she had a man to share it with. And she was ever hopeful.

Serena picked up her computer from the table and settled down in the corner of her couch. She needed to relax before heading to bed, so she might as well check out the men who had contacted her on the dating sites she belonged to.

She scrolled through them. One was William, an accountant, who had one child, a boy. The boy lived with his mother and William had him every other weekend. She wasn't sure if she wanted to take on a man with a child, even if he only saw him twice a month. Plus, she'd met up with guys who were divorced and all they did was talk about their ex-wife. Sometimes it was plain that they still loved them. For others, it was obvious the divorce had been acrimonious. Either way, the conversation was boring and she never went on a second date with them.

Another man was into cross-country and downhill skiing and skidooing in the winter, and kayaking, sailing, and waterskiing in the summer. All things outdoors that she liked to do. He had a sense of humour in that his last line was: *I like to hike, so let's build a trail of bliss together.*

Chapter Eight

Saturday morning, Simone, Serena, and Patricia entered the grocery store and grabbed a cart. Simone and Serena had decided to do some Christmas baking with their mother, something they hadn't done together since they were young. They used to bake and decorate cookies for their teachers and classmates and make chocolates for the neighbours, but the sisters outgrew that once they hit their teen years. Patricia had continued to make chocolates and had given them to family and friends as gifts each year.

"What are we baking?" Serena asked.

"We're making classic sugar cookies," Patricia said. "They're the easiest ones to make."

"Are you hinting that we're not good bakers?"

"When was the last time either of you made a cake or pie?"

Simone and Serena looked at each other. "I don't think I have since I was in grade five and I made my own birthday cake," Simone said.

"And it was awful." Serena wrinkled her nose.

"So I got the salt and sugar amounts mixed up. And what about you, Serena? When have you ever baked anything?"

"I find the cakes and pies in the stores are really good."

"I rest my case," Patricia grinned. She looked at her list. "Now we need butter, flour, sugar, cornstarch, and salt for the cookies. And I'd like to also make some cupcakes to take to the residents at Arbutus Hall this afternoon. Those I will make from a mix but I need cocoa and icing sugar for the icing and some sprinkles."

They wandered the aisles picking up the ingredients needed for the cookies and cupcakes. Simone and Serena also slipped some bread, sandwich meat, cheese, and tomatoes into the cart.

"Our lunch," Simone said.

A tall, older man walked towards them. He stopped in front of Patricia. "Good morning."

"Hello, Roger. How are you today?"

"Just fine."

"Do you remember my daughters, Simone and Serena?"

"Hello, Mr. Wilson," Simone said. "I haven't seen you since you and your wife moved away."

"Well, my wife died and I moved back to the neighbourhood." He looked at the groceries in the cart and then at Patricia. "Do you cook?"

"No," she said quickly. "These are for Serena."

"Then you're no good to me." He turned and walked away.

"What was that about?" Simone asked. She stared after him.

"I've heard via the grapevine that he's looking for another wife."

"Then that was the worst pick-up line ever," Serena muttered.

"You wouldn't believe the number of male friends who are now widowers and have propositioned me," Patricia said with disgust. "And not in a nice way. Dave Canfield told me he needs someone to clean his house and was I interested in moving in. Tom Devens wondered if I would come over and do his laundry for him and maybe provide some female companionship while waiting for it to dry."

"Our mother, the femme fatale," Serena laughed.

"Oh, yes, I've won them over with my seductive powers. That's why they want me to be their live-in maid with benefits."

They paid for their groceries and headed home. While Simone and Serena took everything out of the bags, Patricia put on Christmas music and went to the cupboard for her recipe card box. She looked through the cards and found one. "Here's the recipe for sugar cookies."

Patricia placed a card with her precise handwriting on it on the kitchen counter. "You can get started while I check my emails."

Simone picked up the card and read how much of each item they needed. She took a large bowl from the cupboard and set it on the counter beside the card. "Should we make a double batch, so we can each take some to share with our employees?"

"Sure. Mine will be happy to get something homemade rather than bought from a store. They know I'm really a failure at baking so they might not even believe I actually made them."

Serena used the electric beater to cream the butter while Simone measured and added each of the other ingredients. While they worked Simone told Serena about the conversation she'd had with their mother about Bert.

"I called Raymond and gave him what little information I had on Bert and asked him to find out more if he could."

"How long will that take?" Serena glopped the dough onto a piece of waxed paper and formed it into a long roll. She wrapped the paper around the dough and rolled it on the counter to even it out.

"He said he'd get back to me next week."

"How is it going?" Patricia asked as she entered the kitchen.

The sisters jumped.

"Just about finished," Serena said quickly. She unwrapped the roll and began to cut slices off it and set them on the cookie sheet.

Simone took a fork and poked three rows of holes in the top of the cookies. When two sheets were full, she put them in the heated oven.

"While you're cleaning up, I'll start the cupcakes," Patricia said.

Simone and Serena washed and dried their bowls and utensils while their mother poured the two cake mixes into a bowl and added the eggs and water. She took the beaters and put them back in the mixer and beat the ingredients together.

"Where are your muffin pans?" Simone asked.

"Bottom drawer of the stove."

Simone took the pans out and put the fluted baking cups in each of the holes. She set them beside her mother.

"So you've hired the Webster Private Detective Agency to check out Bert," Patricia said as she concentrated on spooning up some batter into the cups.

Simone glanced at Serena. "Good hearing," she mouthed.

Serena nodded.

"I did ask Raymond to look into Bert's history." Simone spoke slowly, not sure how she should answer.

"Why?"

"We want to make sure you don't get hurt," Serena said as she took the cookie sheets out of the oven.

"Hurt? How?" Patricia carried the muffin pans to the stove. She put them on the rack and closed the oven door. She turned and faced her daughters.

"We're not sure. It's just that you are a rich widow and a lot of men would like to help you spend your money," Simone said.

"Don't you trust me to be able to figure that out myself?" Patricia started to clean up the counter.

"Sometimes we can be blinded by our feelings." Simone thought about Griffin and how her love had blinded her to his sexual orientation.

"I think I've had enough experience, both in real life and in my writing, to look after my own love life." Patricia's voice seethed. "I don't need my daughters telling me what to do."

"We're not trying to tell you what to do." Serena held her hands up.

"Then tell that detective to stop his investigation in Bert."

"I will," Simone said.

"Good. Now let's have lunch."

They prepared their sandwiches and made small talk as they ate. Simone told them that she and Griffin had hired a real estate agent to sell the condo. The agent figured there would be an offer within a few days.

Serena talked about her pub and how hockey season was good for business. "We've been full every evening there's a game."

After putting the food away they worked in silence as they iced the cookies and put sprinkles on them. They divided them three ways. When the cupcakes had cooled, they iced them and placed them in a plastic container.

"You can drop me off at Arbutus Hall," Patricia said to Simone as she put her coat on. She picked up the container. "I'll take a taxi home."

* * *

Serena got in her car and left the yard. Simone closed the passenger door on her mother and climbed in the driver's seat.

"Look, Mom."

"You don't need to say anything more," Patricia said. "The investigation into Bert is over. And I don't want him to ever find out about it. Do you understand?"

"Yes, Mom." Simone felt like she had when she was a child and had done something terribly wrong.

After dropping her mother off, Simone drove to her office. It would be quiet and she had a lot of work to catch up on before heading back to her mother's house. They had another interview this evening with a care giver. Hopefully, they would find one soon.

Simone parked and took the elevator up to her agency. She let herself in and went to her office. She sat down and took out her cell phone. She sent Raymond a text telling him she wished to cancel his investigation into Bert Madden. She would pay for any expenses he might have incurred. Then she opened her email and began going through the latest manuscript synopses the agency had received.

Sometimes, Simone wondered if writers knew just how important a good synopsis was. It had to catch the agent's attention, while giving a quick overview of the plot, characters, theme, conflict, and setting of the story. It had to explain everything major that happened, including the ending. The writer should never suggest that the ending is a surprise; they should tell what the surprise is. Simone had long ago quit reading if someone wrote that she would be shocked at how the story ended when she asked for and read the full manuscript.

At one time, synopses were up to twelve pages long but in the past decade agents and editors began requesting one page single spaced or two pages double spaced. Some even asked that the length be not more than three hundred words. Not much time to hook the agent's interest.

The important thing was for the writer to take their time in crafting the synopsis.

Simone spent the next hour reading three synopses. There was only one that interested her enough to read the first three chapters. She sent that one to her staff to read. She had a rule that at least one other agent had to like the first chapters before asking for the full manuscript.

Her phone pinged. It was from Raymond. *I have some information on Bert Madden if you want it.*

Simone stared at the text. Did she want the information? Her mother had been quite adamant that she had to drop any investigation into Bert. But Raymond had found out this information before Patricia had told Simone to cancel the inquiry so technically...

Simone set Serena a text. *I cancelled the check into Bert but Raymond had already found something. Do we want to know what it is?*

She looked through more of her emails, read the newsletters and new information from the groups she belonged to, and sent the ones from people she didn't know who wanted to be friends on Facebook or LinkedIn or Twitter to trash. She used to check into each person who wanted to be friends on Facebook and usually found that they were a scam. If there were only pictures of the person or ones with dogs and if they had no or few friends, it was easy to see that they were new profiles. She figured that the person would at least have some personal friends or even family members on their sites before contacting strangers.

Her phone pinged. *Tough question. But if we don't tell mom...*

Exactly. Simone sent back.

Yes, I would like that information. Simone typed to Raymond.

Check your email.

Simone brought up her email again. The top one was from Raymond and there was an attachment. Her phoned pinged.

Don't read it without me. I'm on my way to your office.

We have to hurry. Mom will be getting home soon.

Simone had to find out how much she owed Raymond so she could pay him. If he'd sent the information in the attachment, then she was fine. If it was part of the email and his bill was attached, then she would have to look at it without Serena. Plus, she wanted to print a copy for each of them. She opened the email. Raymond had added his invoice in the body. Simone clicked on the attachment.

It showed a two-page document with Bert Madden's name at the top. Without reading it she sent it to the printer. After reading so many manuscripts on her computer every day, Simone preferred to have a paper report. It was easier on her eyes to read and she could shift from one page to the other quicker.

Chapter Nine

Serena hurried out to her car. She had mixed feelings about sneaking behind her mother's back but with Patricia being a rich widow, it was up to her and Simone to look after her and her activities, both financial and physical.

Traffic was light and she arrived at Simone's office building in twenty minutes. She hurried up to the third floor and found the door to the Bell Literary Agency open. She entered.

"I'm here."

"At my desk."

Serena sat in the chair across from Simone. "So, let's see it."

Simone handed her two pages.

They each read them silently.

His occupation was listed as optometrist—he'd had his own company for twenty years and sold it seven years ago and retired at the age of sixty-five. His marital status was widower. His financial status showed a healthy portfolio of investments and two bank accounts.

"It gives his wife's first name as Della and that she died four years ago. I wonder what from," Serena mused. "Was it a suspicious death?"

"You read too many mystery and true crime novels."

"Don't forget all the true crime shows and podcasts. It's amazing how many innocent looking people will kill for money or revenge or love. And why two bank accounts?"

"I have two accounts, one personal with Griffin and one for my business."

"But his wife is dead and he's retired. Maybe he has a mistress somewhere or a secret child and uses one of the accounts to keep the mistress in furs or to pay child support."

"He's in his seventies. He could live with the mistress. And his child should be a grown-up by now."

"Men can have children in their seventies. Mick Jagger fathered a son when he was seventy-three, Tony Randall fathered a daughter when he was seventy-seven and a son when he was seventy-eight."

"How do you know these things?"

Serena shrugged. "I like reading odd things."

"You certainly do. And your memory is superb."

"Yes, for trivial things. Other times I forget an important appointment."

"Bert had two hip replacements, a back operation, and almost died from pneumonia just after he retired."

"Seems pretty normal for a man his age," Serena said. "I don't see anything more about his wife?"

"I cut Raymond's search short. He might not have had time to find out much."

"I'd like to know more about his wife, though. And, does he have children, grandchildren?"

"There's so much we need to know," Simone said.

"We could ask Mom."

"And have her accuse us of meddling in her love life?"

"Really, it's not looking into him if you ask Raymond to find out more about his wife, so you wouldn't be going against Mom's wishes. And if Raymond happens to learn about any children or grandchildren and the bank accounts, that's not our fault."

Simone grinned. "And Mom says we wouldn't make good criminals. I'll ask him to find out what he can on Mrs. Madden."

"Do you have to pick Mom up?" Serena asked.

"No. She insisted she would take a taxi home."

Serena grimaced. "She was still that mad when you dropped her off?"

"I don't blame her," Simone admitted. "No one wants their decisions questioned, especially by their children."

"But if he's going to be our step-dad..." She stopped and grinned. "I wonder if they're having sex right now."

"Serena!"

"What? She said he was good in bed."

"I have to get going to Mom's. Are you coming over?"

"Don't want to face her alone?" Serena grinned.

"We have another interview this evening and we should discuss when we're going to VanDusen gardens. After all, you told mom we'd take her."

"Yes, would going Monday evening work for you?"

"Griffin and I are seeing the lawyer Monday morning to sign paperwork, so I'll need a distraction in the evening."

"How are you doing?"

"It's strange, but I still have feelings for him. I find myself thinking that I have to remember to tell him something or I wonder what he wants for dinner."

"I'm sorry you're going through this. I wish I could do something for you."

"Having Mom to think about and you being around does help." Simone picked up her purse.

"I'll meet you there," Serena said.

Half an hour later Serena pulled into her mother's yard. The lights were all on in the house. She entered and found Simone and Patricia sitting in the living room with another woman. She had blonde hair styled in a bob and wore what looked like a pink nursing uniform and white socks. She had a black purse beside her.

"Serena, this is Candace Monroe, Candace my sister Serena."

Candace stood and held out her hand. "I've apologized to your mother and sister for being early and now I apologize to you. I had an unexpected call to go to a client's house this evening and I sent a text to Simone asking if, instead of cancelling our meeting, I could come now."

"I sent you a text," Simone said.

"My phone did ding, but I was driving and I didn't check. I'm okay with doing the interview now."

"Thank you." Candace smiled as she and Serena sat down. "I've already given Simone and Patricia my references and the list of chores I'm willing to do."

Simone handed the list and references to Serena and she scanned it while Simone and Candace talked. The chores were the same as Ellie's. The references were names of families she had worked for in the past year.

"When would you be able to start?" Serena asked.

Candace looked at Patricia and smiled. "One of my clients, who I've looked after for the past two years, has just gone into assisted living, so I have an opening right now. How often would you want me to come?"

"Three days a week to begin with," Simone said. "Maybe more often if things work out."

"That would be fine with me. I have two clients who I visit in the evenings."

"And I would want you to wear regular clothes, not a uniform," Patricia said.

"I most certainly can do that. I don't really like dressing this way. This is left over from when I worked in a long term care facility before setting out on my own. Some families think a uniform is more clinical and professional."

"Thank you, Candace," Simone said standing. "I will let you know this week."

"Excellent. Goodbye, Patricia. It was nice meeting you."

Simone and Serena followed her to the door and said their goodbyes.

"What do you think?" Simone asked.

"She certainly talks a lot. But what I liked was that she looked at mom a lot, including her in the conversation even though we were the ones talking to her."

"Yes, I noticed that, too. Let's see what Mom says."

They walked back into the living room. Patricia had stood and was headed to the kitchen.

"What's your opinion of Candace, Mom," Serena asked as they followed her.

"I like her. She seems to have a lot of energy. She was telling Simone and me about how she takes her clients shopping, to the Pacific National Exhibition in the summer, to movies, and down to the beach."

Simone's phone pinged. She looked at it. "Well, that's from Nicole. She has found a new client and is cancelling our meeting tomorrow evening. So, it's just between Candace and Ellie."

"My preference is Candace," Patricia said.

"Okay. I'll contact her references tomorrow. If they give her the thumbs up, I'll call her and see if she can start some day start next week."

* * *

Monday morning Simone sat in the waiting room at the lawyer's office. She'd dropped Patricia off at Serena's pub before coming here. Traffic was light and she'd arrived a little early. She couldn't believe how nervous she was. It was one week since she'd moved out of the condo, yet it felt like eons had passed since she'd last seen Griffin.

She checked her cell phone for the time. Ten minutes to two. The time seemed to be dragging. There were nothing to read and she'd checked the name of the artist on every painting on the walls.

The door opened and she automatically looked up. At first she didn't recognize her husband. Gone were the baggy khaki pants and dull gray shirts he generally wore. In their place were slim fitting black jeans, a burgundy bulky sweater over a black shirt the tails of which peeked out at the hem, and a gray cashmere coat. A knitted plaid scarf was loosely knotted around his neck. Slung over his shoulder was a brown messenger bag that matched his shiny leather shoes.

His hair was short at the sides with the longer top slicked back. It had been dyed silver. And he had plucked his bushy eyebrows. His face lit up when he saw her. She noticed that his walk was different as he headed towards her his arms out to hug her. Simone stood and hesitated about embracing him. He looked so very unlike her husband of just a week ago. But she had no choice. He pulled her to him.

She wrapped her arms around him and the desire to continue holding him was strong. She had gone through a gauntlet of emotions since moving out: hurt, anger, resentment, sadness, grief, indignation, and yes, even love and desire and longing. They had been married three years and had made so many memories together. Who would she talk with about their trip to Hawaii, or who would laugh with her at the memory of them getting lost on a hike in the mountains and being found by a gold prospector?

He let go and stood back. Before he could say anything the secretary called to them.

"Mr. and Mrs. Watson, Ms. Cote is ready to see you."

They followed her into an office and sat on the two chairs in front of the desk. Anna Cote looked up and smiled at them.

"Thank you both for coming. This won't take very long since everything is pretty straight forward. I've talked with each of you by phone and I've prepared all the necessary documents as requested. I have them here for you to sign."

She laid the papers in front of them and explained what they were and where each was to sign. "Now you can find a realtor and list your condo, unless one of you wants to buy the other one out."

Simone looked at Griffin. That was something she hadn't thought about. Did she want to live there alone with all the memories of their life together? Did he?

"I'm okay with selling it," Griffin said. "I have other plans."

"Yes, me too." Simone stood.

They shook hands with Anna and left the office.

"I'll meet you at the realtors," Simone said as they rode the elevator down to street level.

"If you don't mind, could you give me a ride? I sold my car and bought a bicycle, but I caught the bus to get here."

"It looks as if you made a lot of changes in your life. I like your new look."

"Thank you. I had a little help, but I think it suits me."

Simone unlocked her car and they climbed in. She drove the five blocks to the real estate company in a building on the corner and parked in their lot. It only took them fifteen minutes to fill out the forms. Simone handed over her key for the realtor to put in the lock box, since she had no plans on ever returning to the condo.

"Would you like to go for a drink?" Griffin asked as they left the building.

"Sure." Simone looked up and down the street. "Let's go to that pub across the street."

They waited for the walk sign to come on and crossed to the other corner. They entered the pub and found a table. The server came over with menus and asked if they wanted something to drink.

"I'll have a Mai Tai," Griffin said.

"And I'll have a six ounce house wine."

The server nodded and left.

Simone opened the menu. It was close to dinner time, but she didn't want to drink on an empty stomach. "Let's order some hummus and pita bread."

"That sounds good."

The server returned with their drinks and took their food order.

Griffin lifted his glass. "I want to thank you for forcing me to admit to everyone who I really am. I was so tired of pretending. You have given me a free life."

Simone slowly lifted her glass to his. She didn't know what to say to that, so she took a sip of her wine.

"You certainly have changed your appearance."

"This is the real me. When I saw the pictures and knew that our marriage was over and so was my charade, I went shopping."

"It does suit you."

"Thank you," Griffin beamed.

Simone smiled. He'd always liked compliments. "In the lawyer's office, you said you have plans. Care to share them?"

"Yes." Griffin leaned forward on the table.

Simone cringed at the memory of how she had enjoyed watching his face light up when he got excited while talking about something new he wanted to try or had heard about. He used to remind her of an eager child.

"Not all the evenings I went out were with friends. I also was taking an evening course at a community college."

Simone remembered something in Raymond's report about him following Griffin to a college, but she hadn't thought much of it figuring that was where Griffin was meeting his boyfriend that evening.

"A course in what?"

"Travel and tourism. I want to work on a cruise ship." He sat back, a big grin on his face.

Simone stared at him. "When did you decide that?" It had to have been months ago.

He at least had the decency to look a little uncomfortable as he realized what she'd meant with her question. "I wasn't going behind your back. It was something I wanted to look into and I didn't want to tell you until I knew if I liked it and wanted to pursue it. I...I wanted to surprise you." He finished lamely.

"Well, it would have been a surprise," Simone said dryly. "Almost as much of a surprise as finding out you were cheating."

Griffin looked down at his glass. "There is no excuse for what I did."

The server set the plate of hummus and pita triangles in the centre of the table and put small plates in front of them. "Would either of you like another drink?"

"Another Mai Tai."

"Nothing for me." Simone spooned some hummus onto her plate and took two triangles. "What other plans have you made?" she asked as she dipped a pita in the hummus.

"I've quit my job. I'm going to see my parents in Nova Scotia soon and tell them about us and admit who I really am. And I've broken it off with Harry. He's also decided to tell his family."

Simone wanted to ask what he was going to do for money but decided it wasn't her place anymore to ask personal questions. There had been a few thousand dollars left in their account when she'd removed her half, plus he'd sold his car. "I guess we should close out our joint account."

"Do you mind if I just keep it open for my use?" Griffin helped himself to some pita and hummus.

"Do you trust me that much?" Simone teased.

"I've known you for years. I know I can trust you."

Simone felt sad that she couldn't say the same anymore about him.

"How is your mother?"

"She's doing okay. I'm staying with her for a while."

"I know she and your sister don't like me much, but say 'Hello' to them for me."

"I will and speaking of Mom, I should get going. Do you need a ride somewhere?"

"No, thank you. I'm getting to know the bus routes and bike lanes quite well. And I'll pay for this." He pulled a wallet out of his bag and laid some cash on the table.

They walked out together and crossed to the parking lot.

"I know you may not believe it, but I have loved you, in my own way," Griffin said. "We did have fun and a good marriage. And I do apologize for using you and our marriage to hide behind."

Without waiting for a comment, he turned and started towards the street. He stopped after a few steps and looked back. "Since I thought I had to marry a woman, I'm glad I chose you."

Simone watched him leave not sure if that had been a compliment. He had changed since she last saw him a week ago. He was more relaxed, more open. Gone was the tension in his stance, the tightness in his face. She had always wondered why he seemed so rigid even when having a good time and laughing with friends. There had always been a part of him that seemed to hold back from having fun.

He was much happier than she had ever seen him in all the years she knew him.

Chapter Ten

Serena stepped out of her office and went to the lounge to check up on her mother. The lunch crowd had come and gone and the place was quieter. Only five tables were in use. The servers were cleaning and resetting the other tables for the evening meal. Patricia was in what seemed to be her favourite spot, behind the counter with Lenny. They were laughing and from her mother's pose, Serena thought she was again flirting with him.

Once more, Serena wondered if her mother had had extramarital affairs. Patricia had always been outgoing and when Serena occasionally attended one of her parents' parties she could remember her mother talking and laughing with the men more than with the women. Patricia had left the women for Craig. And he had risen to the occasion, telling them stories about his work or the recent trips he had been on, or, being an avid sports fan, giving his opinion about the last hockey or football game he had attended.

Hell, had her father had any affairs? She'd never thought of her parents having sex with each other let alone with someone else. But it was a total possibility, maybe even a necessity on her mother's part, so she could write her steamy sex scenes.

"Hello, Dear," Patricia said when Serena reached them.

"I hope you haven't been pestering Lenny." She looked at Lenny who shook his head.

"No. In fact he's been helping me with some research for my novel."

"Oh?"

"Yes. One of my characters owns a bar and Lenny's been explaining the different parts of the bar, or in your pub's case, counter, since people don't really come here to order an alcoholic drink. He also said that an establishment called a bar is licensed to serve alcohol beverages and is named after the bar," here she paused and slapped the top of the counter. "on which the drinks are served, while the name 'pub' is short for Public House. Back in the old days, like centuries ago in Britain, the brewer of ale would hang a bush above his door to let people know his place was a public drinking establishment and not a private one. The first pubs in Britain were really Roman taverns that sold alcoholic drinks and food."

Patricia smiled at Lenny. "See, I was paying attention."

"You're a quick study." Lenny winked.

Was Lenny actually flirting back? "What else did you learn?"

"There are three sections to the counter: the front counter, back counter, and under counter. The front counter is where the servers come to give the drink orders. The back counter is at the back of the front counter and is the place where the beverage server does all their work. In the case of a bar, there would be a display rack of all the liquor bottles along the wall behind the bartender. Here, you have before and after pictures of your pub, posters, a few antique bottles, and plants. There is a sink for rinsing glasses and anything off their hands. And the third part, the under counter, is self-explanatory."

"You did learn a lot."

"Yes, and now I must type it all into my story before I forget it." Patricia went around the counter and over to where her computer sat on a small table. She opened it and started typing.

"Thank you for helping her," Serena said.

"She's fun to talk with and I enjoy listening to her stories about the ups and downs of her writing career. Sounds like it's not an easy way to make money."

Serena had never thought about her mother's career. Writing was something that Patricia had always done. She'd never complained about any problems, at least not to her daughters.

Serena walked to her mother's table. "We should be heading to your place soon."

"Any time you're ready." Patricia continued typing.

"I have a few things to do so in about half an hour."

Patricia nodded.

Serena went back to her office to finish her paperwork. She'd just sat down when her burner phone dinged. She saw it was from Albert, a man she'd been texting with for the past two weeks. Until she had found a permanent relationship she was going to keep her options open. She'd contacted Albert last night wondering if he wanted to meet for a drink.

I'm free for dinner tonight.

Busy tonight. She sent back. *What about tomorrow at noon?*

One at O'Hare's?

Yes.

I'll be wearing a Canucks hat.

Serena thought it was weird since they had exchanged pictures of each other. Then she shrugged her shoulders. Maybe he liked showing he was a proud Vancouver Canucks fan or maybe he was bald.

Half an hour later Serena picked up her purse and coat and headed to the lounge. Patricia had closed her computer and placed it in its case. She put on her coat when she saw Serena and the two of them walked out of the pub. Even though it was only four o'clock, it was getting dark and colder. There was a hint of rain in the air.

"I'm picking up dinner, so what would you like?" Serena said as she pulled out into the street.

"Oh, I'll be so glad to have home cooked meals again," Patricia sighed. "Lauren was such a good cook. I hope Candace is, too."

"We never asked her that, did we."

"No, but her chore list did include making meals, so hopefully she is."

"Let's go to Café Gloucester. You like their baked Portuguese chicken with rice."

"Yes, I do," Patricia agreed.

Serena drove to Cambie Street and parked close to the restaurant. They entered and were given the take out menu.

"We'll have the Caesar salad, spaghetti bolognaise, baked prawns with garlic, and baked Portuguese chicken with rice."

"It will be about ten minutes."

"We'll wait." Serena and Patricia sat on the sofa beside the door. They watched customers come and go and were finally called to the desk. Serena paid and they carried the bags to the car.

"We've got dinner," Serena called when they entered the house.

"Coming." Simone appeared in the doorway as Serena set the bags on the counter.

While Serena and Patricia removed their coats, Simone took plates from the cupboard and put them on the island.

"We'll just spoon the food out of the containers," Serena said as she opened the bag. "We should get going to the gardens soon. It's getting cold and looks like rain."

They all quickly dished up.

"How did your meeting with Griffin go?" Serena asked Simone. "Any problems?"

"No, actually it went very well. We're selling the condo and dividing the proceeds equally."

"Even though you put up most of the down payment?" Patricia asked.

"It's not a point worth arguing about. We both just want this over."

"Is he anxious to set up house with his boyfriend?"

"No. He's been taking a course, so that he can work on a cruise ship."

"A cruise ship?" Patricia asked, indignantly. "And he never said anything to you about it? The namby-pamby."

"Namby-pamby?" Serena laughed.

"Poltroon, recreant, lily-liver, coward, which ever you want. He was sneaking behind your back in more ways than one. How did you not know Simone?"

"I did know something was different. That's why I hired a detective."

"How long had you suspected something?" Serena asked.

"About six months, which is the time he started the course and soon after he met his boyfriend."

"And you never told me? Told us?"

"I didn't have anything concrete until Raymond gave me the pictures."

"Did you know there is a dog charity in Vancouver where you can buy a plastic bag filled with dog poo and put the first name of someone you think has been shitty towards you on it." Patricia smiled at Simone.

"And then what do you do with it?" Serena asked. "Take it and leave it on his doorstep or throw it at his front door?"

"No. They display the bags on their front lawn for people to read the names."

"Oh, that's disappointing. I'd want to let him know more forcefully how I felt." Serena looked at Simone and realized the conversation was bothering her. "I'm sorry. We shouldn't be talking about him right now."

"Yes, sorry," Patricia agreed. "I just get so mad when someone takes advantage of either of my girls."

"Griffin did want me to say 'Hello' to both of you."

Serena looked at the clock on the wall. "We should go."

Griffin was not one of her favourite people and like their mother, she thought he'd taken advantage of Simone during their marriage. Now she knew he was dealing with his own problems at the time but that still didn't mean he should have treated Simone so poorly. Nor did it mean that he should have found someone else while still married.

They quickly put the leftover food in the fridge and the dishes in the dishwasher. They found their coats and went out to

Serena's car. VanDusen Botanical Gardens was also on Oak Street but it was too far to walk. Serena turned into the parking lot and drove around. She spied a car with its backup lights on. She waited for it to leave the spot and pulled in.

"Perfect timing," Serena said as she shut off her car. She had booked advance tickets online and they headed to that line. It was shorter and they were soon staring at the tall trees with strings of yellow, blue, red, and green, lights strung from the bottom of their trunks to their tops. Lights stretched into the distance to the left, right, and ahead.

"There are more than one million lights on the trees, bushes, Christmas scenes, and in flower beds," Patricia commented.

"And I thought I liked a lot of lights," Simone said. "This must have taken a long time to decorate."

"You could probably get a part time job here in the fall," Serena smiled. "It would give you your Christmas fix."

"I did some research while at the pub today and this used to be a golf course that opened in 1912," Patricia said as they walked through the crowds of people on the paths. "The gardens opened in 1975 with twelve thousand trees, bushes, and flowers on display. The Festival of Lights began in 1984 and is the city's longest-running holiday occasion." She had to shout to finish the last sentence.

The three strolled the lit and decorated pathways. They dodged the running children, avoided the people who stopped to stare at the dancing lights around Livingstone Lake, and waited for the people who stopped to take pictures. They each lit a candle at the Make-A-Wish Canada Grotto. They walked through the Pink Tunnel where all the lights were pink, went to Candy Cane Lane, and through the Gingerbread Wood. Gnomes, dressed in baggy brown pants and shirts, cream coloured felted vests, and red Phrygian caps, carried large candy canes as they scurried through the crowd, laughing and pausing for pictures.

"I'm getting cold," Patricia said. "Who wants a spiced rum or hot chocolate? I'm buying."

"Me."

"Me."

After they'd had their hot drinks, they continued on one of the paths to the exit and Serena drove them home.

"Do you want to come in?" Simone asked as she opened the passenger door.

"Thanks, but I have to work a few hours yet tonight."

"Good night, then."

"Good night, Simone. Have a good sleep, Mom."

* * *

Patricia went up to her bedroom. After locking the doors and shutting off all the lights, Simone climbed the stairs to hers. It had been a long day and she was thankful for her mother and sister for keeping her distracted this evening. Even though she and Griffin had signed the papers today that would lead to the ending of their marriage she was still having a hard time believing it was happening.

Sure, she'd had her suspicions for half a year and had hired a detective to find out if she was right but truthfully, she'd hoped Raymond would come back with a reasonable explanation, something like Griffin was working overtime and wanted to surprise her with money for a vacation. Deep down, she hadn't wanted to believe that Griffin would cheat on her.

In just one week, he'd been found with another man, she'd moved out, they were selling the condo she thought she'd be living in for years yet, and were headed for a divorce.

Seeing the new Griffin today had been a shock. He was a totally different man in looks and actions. And he had his future all planned out. She hadn't thought beyond today. Mind you, he'd had months to make plans, she was only in her first week.

Simone changed into her nightgown and climbed into bed. She'd shut off her cell phone after leaving Griffin so her evening with her mother and sister wouldn't be interrupted. She turned it back on and there was a lot of pinging as her phone let her know all the messages it had been saving for her.

She scrolled through her texts and found one from Melanie.

I think it's time we had a ladies night out. Plus, I haven't heard from you and I want to know that you are okay.

Could she leave her mother for an evening and go out with a friend? Would Patricia be fine by herself? Should she take the chance? There had been no word about Lauren and she didn't trust that Lauren wouldn't try to contact her mother. Maybe Patricia could spend the evening with Serena. They could go out somewhere together. She sent a text to Serena.

Can mom stay with you tomorrow evening while I go out with Melanie? I could pick her up afterwards.

Yes, I have nothing planned.

Simone sent a heart emoji to Serena then answered Melanie's text.

I'm okay and yes, it's time we met. What about tomorrow evening for dinner and drinks?

She and Melanie had worked together at the literary agency where Simone had learned her trade. They had discussed going into business together but Melanie had become pregnant with twins and decided she wanted to be a stay-at-home mom to her daughter and son. They had maintained their friendship, going out together at least once a month.

Yes! Let's meet at Paul's Seafood and Chop House on Robson at six-thirty.

Perfect.

Simone would have to leave at four-thirty to get her mother to the pub and then drive from the pub to Robson. She sent a text to Serena saying she'd be there at around five with their mother.

Serena sent back a thumbs-up.

Simone looked at her literary agency emails and found fifteen new submissions from writers. With having to keep an eye on her mother and not going into her office very often, she was falling behind in her work. She knew her agents were busy since each one had to make a report on Mondays about which, if any, first chapters they were interested in. She and her agents looked for writers in different genres and among them they covered romance, mystery, fantasy, historical, and young adult. Her agency wasn't interested in children's books, poetry, erotic romance, westerns, Christian, or non-fiction.

Simone yawned as she sent the submissions to the bottom of her to-be-read file. She was tired but didn't think she could sleep. She checked Facebook and Twitter and then played Scrabble. She had seven games going, five with friends and two against the computer. She liked the computer games, they were set so that she won most of them. Her friends were not so considerate.

After the last game, Simone picked up the latest book she was reading. She liked to read, maybe that was why she liked being a literary agent. She got to read the beginning of a lot of different stories for free. If she liked the beginning she then was able to read the rest of the manuscript. The one thing she didn't like was reading them all on computer. She preferred a paper book. It wasn't as hard on her eyes.

After she'd read a couple of chapters she felt sufficiently tired to go to sleep. She closed the book and shut the light off.

* * *

Serena had used the voice-to-text feature on her vehicle phone to answer Simone's request. She was glad her sister was going out with Melanie. Simone needed to get back into normal life. Living with their mother and spending most of her time looking after her was not something she should be doing now. That would come later when their mother was incapable of looking after herself. Maybe they should have hired Candace to start immediately instead of next week. It would have made Simone's life much easier.

The burner phone in her purse pinged. Someone was interested in her profile. She wasn't sure if that was a good thing anymore. So far none of the men she'd met were ones she would take home to meet her mother. Once in her parking lot, she took the phone out of her purse and looked at the message.

I'm back in town for two days. Can we meet tomorrow evening for dinner if you are free? Perry.

She hadn't thought about Perry in a couple of weeks. They'd met three times and then two months ago he said he had to go away on business and wasn't sure how long he'd be gone. There hadn't been any texts from him since he left so she'd written him off as another ship passing in the dark.

She was about to answer yes when she remembered her texts with Simone.

Sorry, I'm spending the evening with my mother.

It would be an opportunity for me to meet her.

Meeting parents was usually reserved until a relationship was serious. Did he think that way, that the two of them were serious? Since she hadn't heard from him in the time he was gone she doubted it. And she also doubted that he cared for her so much that he was willing to meet her mother just to spend time with her.

She'd been away from work too much lately, so she agreed with a stipulation. *Okay but it has to be at my pub.*

I'll be there at six.

Serena sent a thumbs up and headed into her pub. It was Ethan's evening to work but he had asked if he could leave at ten. She had agreed, thinking she would tend the bar instead of asking Lenny if he wanted to work the four hours on his day off.

The lounge was full of talk and laughter from the men and women watching the hockey game between the Canucks and Edmonton Oilers. It was near the end of the third period and they were tied at two goals. Serena waved at Ethan and Arleth then carried her purse to her office. She went to the bathroom and scrubbed her hands in the sink. She insisted that all her staff wash their hands often during their shift and had sanitizer under the counter for them to use when necessary.

She went to the kitchen to make sure things were going smoothly then headed into the lounge and walked behind the counter.

"Thank you for the time off," Ethan said as he rinsed his hands in the sink.

"You're welcome." She liked Ethan, liked all her staff, in fact. They seemed to enjoy working for her and were always willing to work extra shifts or help with any special occasions she planned, like the parking lot barbeque she'd held last July to raise money for the food bank.

Serena slipped Ethan's order pad into her pocket, picked up two menus, and grabbed a tray. She went to a table of four and gathered up the empty glasses and bottles. She set the menus on the table. "Would you like to order something to eat, maybe wings or ribs?" She liked to encourage her evening customers to eat while they drank so they didn't get too drunk.

"We'll have two more beers and two ciders," one of the men said while the women opened the menus.

"Be right back."

Serena went behind the counter and put the bottles in the half empty box and set the glasses in the sink. She opened the cooler and took out the beer and ciders. She popped the tops off the bottles, set them and glasses on the tray, and went back to the table.

"We'll have four tiny tuna tacos, an order of potstickers, and one of dry ribs," one of the women said.

Serena wrote the items on the order pad, then tore it off and went into the kitchen. She hung the paper on the carousal and left. A few minutes later she went back and loaded the plates on the tray along with four smaller plates. She carried them to the table. There was no need to remember who had wanted what like she would have to do if they each had ordered a dish. These were finger foods that they would all share. She set the food plates in the centre of the table and placed a small plate in front of each of them.

There were whoops and hollers from the crowd as a Canuck player skated one on one towards the Edmonton goalie, then a bunch of awwws as the goalie made a spectacular save and gloved the puck.

The hockey game went into overtime and many of the customers asked for their bills. They stayed to watch the overtime but when the Canucks scored in the first five minutes, the lounge mostly cleared out. After all, many of them had to work tomorrow.

The ones who remained continued drinking and eating for the pub stayed open for another two hours. She didn't expect any new customers to come in at this late hour.

Serena had time to wipe off the counter and take the used glasses to the kitchen. She restocked the cooler with bottles of beer and cider. Then she helped Arleth clean off the empty tables and carry the dirty dishes to the kitchen for the washing staff. They reset the tables with cutlery and napkins for lunch tomorrow.

Arleth got a sanitizing spray and wiped the menus.

At two in the morning, she said goodbye to Arleth and the kitchen staff and locked the door behind them. She walked through the lounge looking for any last minute things that needed tidying. Everything looked fine. She retrieved her purse and turned out the lights. She unlocked the door, went out and relocked it behind her. A couple of minutes more and she was throwing her purse on her kitchen table and dropping on her couch.

What a long day. She hoped she could sleep in tomorrow.

Chapter Eleven

The lunch rush was almost over. Most of the regulars were leaving to go back to their jobs while a few, who had a later lunch hour, were trickling in. Serena carried two plates to a table and set them down in front of the customers. She topped up their water glasses and asked if they wanted anything more. They both shook their heads.

Serena went to the next table and stacked the dirty dishes to carry to the kitchen. She backed to the swinging door and pushed it open with her hip. She set the dishes on the counter by the sink for the washers to scrape off and put in the dishwasher. When she'd cleaned and reset the empty tables, Serena went to her office.

She paid some bills, made up a bank deposit, and placed an order for more cider. She walked to the bank and deposited her bag then removed some money from the ATM machine. It was time she did some Christmas shopping.

Back in the pub Serena checked to make sure everything was running smooth then went to her Prius. Until 2020, she had purchased most of her Christmas gifts for family and friends at Ten Thousand Villages on Granville Island. She had liked their uniqueness and the fact that she was helping artisans in impoverished countries. But in 2020 most of the villages closed in Canada. There were now only four left and one of them was in Abbotsford, an hour's drive away.

She looked at the clock on her dash. It was almost two. She would get there by three, traffic permitting. Shop for at least an hour, and then another hour home. She'd get back at five at the earliest. That was cutting it too close. She could do her shopping next week but she wanted to give her employees a cash bonus and a wrapped gift early, so they could use the money for their own Christmas shopping or whatever they wished.

However, it was only a thirty minute drive to Granville Island. If she left now she would have time to visit many of the artisan shops and boutiques and find something appropriate for each employee and get back in time. Then she had another idea.

I'm going shopping on Granville Island, so I'll pick up Mom around five on my way home. She sent Simone.

Works for me.

Serena started her vehicle and left the parking lot. She now had just over two hours to shop. And, since she'd already thought of a few items that each employee might like, she should get it all done.

Traffic was steady on Granville Street, also known as Highway 99, which lead directly to where she had to turn off and drive under the Granville Bridge to the island. Parking was always hard to find and she had to drive around for ten minutes before finding a place. Luckily, it was easy to walk from shop to shop on the island. She enjoyed the Christmas lights and holiday music that played from the stores as she walked by.

Lenny, Arleth, and Ethan had worked for her since she opened her pub and she was grateful for their support. Her first stop was Alarte Silks where she wandered through the shop looking at the various colorful designs on scarves, shawls, and wraps. Arleth loved wearing scarves and always had one around her neck when she came to work. Serena picked out an original silk and felted wool scarf in blues, greens, and magenta colours with a matching felted wool pin. One down.

Serena looked at a few other scarfs and shawls thinking of her mother but decided to wait until closer to Christmas to buy gifts for her family.

Her next stop was the Arts Club Theatre Company. Ethan was a struggling actor who auditioned for as many shows as possible, usually in smaller theatres. He often talked wistfully of getting a part in one of the shows put on in the Arts Club Theatre, but he felt he didn't have the acting credits needed to even try for a lesser part. Serena figured he might enjoy tickets to three shows coming in the New Year.

Lenny was easier to buy for. He liked anything wrought iron, showing her pictures of his latest purchase like a mirror with a wrought iron frame or a wrought iron garden sculpture for his deck.

Serena went to B.C. Blacksmith Inc. and wandered around looking at candle holders and sculptures of an octopus, a cyclist, and even a witch. She finally settled on a wall mounted, wine holder that held ten bottles. Three done.

There was a turnover of her kitchen staff as they each found a job in a more prestigious restaurant in Vancouver or some other city. The pub was only a work experience for them. She bought gift cards to the Keg for each of the kitchen staff and for Noah since he had only been working for her for three months.

All her staff would receive bonuses according to how long they had worked.

Serena looked at her cell phone. Time to pick up her mother. She walked back to her vehicle with her packages and put them in the back. She was just about to climb in the front when someone called her name.

"Serena!"

She turned and sighed. She thought about getting in and driving away then changed her mind. "Hello, Darren."

"My offer is still open."

"Offer?"

"Yes. I still want to get back together."

"Well, I don't. In fact, I have a date this evening and I have to go get ready." Serena climbed into the driver's seat and locked the door. She backed out of the parking space and drove away without looking at Darren. Maybe now he would get the message.

Patricia and Simone were in the living room having a glass of wine. Patricia was dressed in a pantsuit and had her coat beside her on the couch. Simone wore a red dress and had blow dried her hair, so it had some body. She'd even applied make-up, something Serena hadn't seen her do since she'd found out about Griffin.

"Would you like a glass?" Simone asked.

"No, thank you. I have to get back to the pub soon." She decided not to tell Simone about her date. There was no way she was going to let her sister change her plans.

Christmas music was playing and the Christmas tree was lit up. There were a few wrapped presents under it.

"Has Santa come early?" Serena took off her coat and walked over to the tree.

"Those are the gifts I bought with Lauren," Patricia said. "And don't either of you think about shaking them or trying to carefully unwrap them like you used to do as kids. I could always tell."

"I still remember the year Serena and I each snuck one of our gifts upstairs to my bedroom and opened them," Simone laughed. "You had put a pair of Dad's old socks in mine."

"And I found old magazines in mine," Serena grinned sitting down on the couch beside her mother. "We were shocked and then we realized we hadn't ever fooled you. That was the last year we let our curiosity get the better of us."

"I miss those Christmases when you girls were young," Patricia said. "They were so much fun. Your Dad always looked forward to eating the cookies you made Christmas Eve day to leave for Santa."

"They didn't always turn out the way they should," Serena smiled. "Like the year we burned them and didn't have time to make more."

"Yes, well, he did his best to eat those ones, but finally had to throw them away."

They talked and laughed about a few more Christmas stories and then Serena finally had to say. "We should get going."

"I'm ready." Patricia picked up her coat.

Serena helped her put it on and grabbed her own. "Have a good time this evening," she said to Simone.

"Thank you. I'll text you when I'm on my way to pick Mom up."

"No hurry. The whole kitchen needs cleaning, so that will keep her busy."

"Serena!" Patricia scolded.

"Okay." Serena opened the door. "You only have to wash the dirty pots and pans to pay for your meal."

"Humph," Patricia said as they walked out of the house. "Simone said you were Christmas shopping on Granville Island this afternoon."

"Yes. I bought my staff a few things." She opened the car door for her mother. Once Patricia was settled she closed the door and went around to the driver's side.

"Speaking of staff, is Lenny working this evening?" Patricia asked as Serena pulled out of the driveway.

"Are you sweet on him?" Serena smirked as she used one of the older era phrases like Patricia often did.

"He's way too young for me," Patricia scoffed. "He's just a nice man to talk to. I'm sure you've noticed that."

"Yes, you're right he is. But I'm afraid it's his night off."

"Oh."

"But don't you worry. Your night will be exciting because you're having dinner with my date and me."

"I'm what?"

"I have a date this evening and he wants you to join us."

"Oh, I'm sure he does," Patricia said dryly.

"He does, actually. When I said I couldn't meet him tonight because I would be with you, he said he would like to meet you."

"How serious is this and how come I haven't heard about him before?"

"It's definitely not serious. We saw each other three times last summer and then he left on business two months ago and this is the first I've heard from him since. Besides, he's leaving again in two days."

"So it's a booty call."

"What?" Serena gaped at her mother. "No!"

"Then why else would he contact you and agree for me to come. He's trying to get on your good side and into your pants."

"We never had sex on any of our dates so he certainly can't be expecting it this time."

"Maybe he wants a three-some."

"Mom!"

"What? I've done it before."

Oh, my god. Why was her mother telling her all this? It certainly wasn't something she wanted to know.

"Your father and I did some experimenting in our younger years. Remember I was born in the fifties and grew up in the sixties part of the '*don't make war, make love*' generation. How do you think I was able to write about it in my books?"

"Your imagination?" Serena gulped.

"I've told you before my imagination will only take me so far. You've heard Simone talk about that saying for writers that they should write about what they know. Well, that's what I go by."

Serena was at a loss for words. She and Simone had been surprised that Patricia was visiting Bert for sex, but she had thought it was just normal sex. Thinking about what else they may be doing shocked her. Maybe having Patricia tag along on her date wasn't the best idea. Time to change the subject.

"You said you think you're too old to be writing young love stories. Have you thought about older love stories? You've certainly done a lot of research."

Patricia looked at Serena and grinned. "I hadn't thought about it, but I do have the experience. I'll have to talk with my agent about it."

Serena pulled into her parking space and she and Patricia went up to her condo. She wondered if she should dress up for her meal with Perry. The first time they'd met had been for a walk along False Creek. He had dressed in gray cargo shorts and a white tee. Their second date was to a movie with dinner afterwards. He'd looked smart in his tan slacks, blue shirt, and tan jacket. Perry was a successful businessman but he didn't flaunt it. He drove a three year old BMW convertible but also had a four-wheel drive Jeep. On one date they'd explored lot of gravel roads in the Cultus Lake area and had a picnic overlooking the lake. Then he'd gone on his trip and she hadn't heard from him for months.

"What are you going to wear tonight?" Patricia asked.

"I thought I would go as I am."

Patricia wrinkled her nose. "Really? Jeans and a sweater?"

"We're meeting in my pub not a seven star restaurant."

"There's no such thing as a seven star restaurant."

"Yes, there is. The Al Iwan restaurant is in the Burj Al Arab hotel in Dubai, United Arab Emirates. The hotel is the only seven star hotel in the world and so, therefore, is the Al Iwan."

Patricia waved her hand in dismissal. "Now you're just being muddle-headed."

"What?"

"You're being silly.

Serena decided to ignore that. "He's just looking for someone to spend time with. And for some reason he chose me. And you."

"Well, you could change into a dress or something more formal. You never know where this could lead."

"I'm not sure if I want it to lead anywhere. We had fun on our dates but there didn't seem to be anything between us."

"Love at first sight or love on first date is very rare. Sometimes you have to let it build."

"Let's just say I didn't miss him while he was gone, but I will change to keep you happy."

"That's my girl," Patricia smiled.

Half an hour later, Serena sat at a table wearing black slacks and a pink silk blouse. She had brushed her hair and sprayed it to keep it in place and, like her sister, had put on a little make-up.

Christmas music played softly while the televisions showed the Hero World Challenge golf tournament in Albany, Bahamas.

"What does he look like?" Patricia asked, glancing around the room.

Serena took out her cell phone and scrolled through her pictures until she found one of her and Perry on their picnic. She showed it to her mother.

"He's a nice looking man. He must work out judging from the size of his arms."

"Yes, he goes to the gym a couple of times a week."

"Hello, Serena."

Serena looked up to see Perry standing by the table. She hadn't even seen him come in.

"And you must be Serena's mother." He bowed slightly.

"Yes, I'm Patricia." She held out her hand to shake his but instead he raised it to his lips for a kiss. "Oh, my. A proper, genteel young man."

"I'm Perry. It's so very nice to meet you." He sat in the chair beside her and across from Serena.

Well, Serena now knew for sure that he had just wanted to spend time with someone while in the city. She wondered how many of his friends and acquaintances had turned him down before she'd agreed.

Noah came over with menus and waited while they decided on what to drink.

"I'll have a beer," Perry said.

"I'd like an apple cider," Patricia decided.

"I'll have a cider also." Serena didn't have to drive anywhere this evening since Simone was picking their mother up.

Noah left and they read over the menus.

"How have you been, Serena?" Perry asked.

"Fine.

"How old are you?" Patricia asked Perry, looking up from her menu.

"Oh, um, thirty-four."

"You're a year younger than Serena."

"Yes, almost exactly. Her birthday is on August 10th and mine is August 15th."

"How nice. You could celebrate together."

"Yes, we could."

Serena felt his eyes on her. She glanced up and smiled. She doubted that would happen. "How was your trip?"

"Very good. I'm opening a new office in St. John's, Newfoundland."

"Congratulations."

"I think I'll have the beef dip." Patricia closed her menu. "What type of business are you in?"

"I own a trucking company. We move goods across Canada and into the United States."

"Very impressive." Patricia nodded. "Did you start it yourself?"

"My sister and I did. We each bought a truck and worked for other companies while learning the business. When we thought we were ready we got our own contracts. I opted to work in the office while she wanted to continue driving truck. She's one hell of a driver." He glanced at Patricia. "Excuse my language."

"Excused."

Noah set their drinks on the table and took their food order. Perry wanted the fish and chips and Serena asked for quesadilla. She liked the way Jackson prepared them.

"Do you like sex?" Patricia asked.

"What?"

"Mom!"

"My daughter doesn't like me to talk about sex, even though I write about it all the time. She said you didn't have sex when you two went out. I'm just wondering if you're like my son-in-law."

Perry looked at Serena for help.

"My brother-in-law came out of the closet recently," Serena explained. "It's been a bit of a shock."

"Well, I'm not gay," Perry said to Patricia. He turned to Serena. "And, yes, I like sex with women. I just don't broach the subject until we've dated a few times."

Serena's face was red. She wasn't sure if it was because of Perry looking at her or because of her mother's directness. Maybe she should call Lenny and get him to come in to work. Right now she'd be willing to pay him double overtime to keep her mother occupied.

"Are you good in bed?"

This time Perry smiled a little. He seemed to have adjusted to the interrogation. "I like to think so."

"My husband was good in bed. We were good in bed together. I liked to pull the occasional surprise on him, too. One time before we were married I showed up at his house wearing just a long coat. When he opened the door I opened the coat. And a couple of times I jumped out of our closet naked after we were married. Scared and tantalized him at the same time."

"Sounds like you had a wonderful marriage."

"Yes, we did." Patricia rapidly blinked her eyes to keep the tears from falling.

Serena hoped her mother wouldn't tell him what she'd revealed earlier about her parents' sex life. She sighed in relief when Noah delivered their food.

"Well, let's dig in," she said with false heartiness. She wondered how she could quickly end this date without sounding rude.

Chapter Twelve

Simone said goodbye to Melanie and headed to her car. She had enjoyed the evening, and was a little disappointed that it had to end earlier than expected. Melanie's husband had called and said their son had a fever and was coughing. Being a good mother, Melanie hurried home to be with her son.

But getting out again had made Simone realize how much she missed meeting her friends for a meal or drinks. Since her discovery of Griffin's affair, and the disappearance of Lauren, she'd been spending her time preparing for her divorce, working, or with her mother. She hadn't gone to her Monday night painting class nor to her bowling night. In fact, she hadn't even phoned to say she wasn't attending either.

Simone had to do something to get her life going again. Maybe she should hire someone to stay with her mother, so she could go out in the evenings. She also had to start letting her friends know that she and Griffin were divorcing, for that was another thing she'd quit doing—answering her friends texts and phone calls.

As if on cue, her cell phone dinged. Simone dug it out of her purse. It was a text from Raymond Webster. She opened it.

I have some information about Mrs. Madden. I have to write up the report and figure out the charges. I can email it in the morning.

Okay.

Simone drove to the B&B Pub and entered. She saw Serena and her mother sitting at a table with a handsome man. She walked over.

"Simone, you're earlier than I expected," Serena said. "Join us."

Was that relief in Serena's voice, Simone wondered? She kissed her mother's cheek then sat in the chair across from her.

"Simone, this is Perry, a friend. Perry, my sister Simone."

"Nice to meet you," Simone said, shaking his hand.

"Would you like a drink?" Perry asked.

"No, thank you. I just came from dinner."

"Well, I've had a very delightful evening with your sister and mother."

"You have?" She looked from Perry to Serena. "You two were on a date?"

"Well, kind of...." Serena started to say.

"I'd asked her out and she said she was spending time with your mother, so I said I'd like to meet her."

Simone was confused. Serena hadn't said anything about dating a man named

Perry or that they had been seeing each other long enough that it was time for meeting parents. Why hadn't Serena said she had plans for tonight? Simone could have met up with Melanie some other time.

"Perry and I went on a few dates last summer and then he went to Newfoundland to open a branch of his business there. He phoned me yesterday."

Simone thought she understood. Serena hadn't wanted her to cancel her plans.

"I'm very sorry about you and your husband splitting up," Perry said.

"What?" Simone looked from Serena to her mother. What had they been telling this man?

"Your mother was telling me about you going through a divorce."

"Oh, yes, she's been telling him a lot about our family," Serena said dryly. "Much more than he needed to know."

"There's nothing wrong with what we discussed," Patricia said. "I just told him some of the ways your dad and I kept our marriage exciting."

"And you told him about your brother, Uncle Stan, who resigned from his job because of financial indiscretions and Grandma who worked in a bordello to put herself through nursing school."

Those were stories that had been talked about in whispers at family reunions when the sisters were young. Simone hadn't thought about them for years, not since most of her aunts and uncles had either died or gone into nursing homes and the reunions ended.

"I think I should get you home," Simone said to Patricia. "I've had a long day."

"Okay." Patricia stood.

"Her coat is in my office," Serena said. "I'll go get it."

"We'll get it. You stay here. It was nice meeting you, Perry."

"Hopefully, we can do this again sometime," Perry said.

Simone nodded, not sure what else to say. She had to find out from Serena what exactly had happened tonight. Plus, she had to tell her about Raymond's text. She'd call her later.

"How was your evening with Melanie?" Patricia asked on their way home.

"We had fun but her little boy is sick, so she had to leave early. What do you think of Perry?"

"He's very smart and very successful. But he's not very romantic. They never had sex when they dated last summer."

"He told you this?"

"No, Serena did."

"It doesn't sound like they saw much of each other."

"No, and that's too bad. I think he likes her and she likes him, but his business takes him away a lot."

"If it's meant to be, it will happen."

"Yes."

Simone parked and helped her mother out of the car. After saying goodnight to Patricia, Simone went to her room and immediately called Serena.

She listened while Serena told her about Patricia wondering if Perry wanted a three-some, asking him if he liked sex, wondering if he was like Griffin, and telling him about all the times she'd appeared naked to surprise their father.

"It really was a night from Hell," Serena sighed. "I doubt I'll ever hear from him again."

"Well, I have something that will take your mind off it. I got a text from Raymond and he has some news about Bert's wife. He's emailing it in the morning."

"So where can we meet after you get it?"

"I have to take Mom to her hairdressers at ten tomorrow. From there, I'll go to my office and print it off. I'll meet you at a little café just down the block from the hairdressers. That way I can quickly pick Mom up afterwards."

"Okay."

The next morning Simone dropped Patricia at Francine's Hairstyles. Francine had been Patricia's hairdresser for years at a salon and when she semi-retired she'd decided to work part time out of her home. She only took in friends or friends of friends or previous customers, Patricia being one of them.

The appointment would take about two hours, so from there Simone drove to her office and, after checking with Grace that everything was running smoothly, printed off Raymond's report and put it in a manila envelope. Then she went to the café where Serena was waiting. Two cups of coffee sat on the table. Serena's was almost empty.

As Christmas music played softly in the background, Simone opened the envelope. She spread the two sheets on the table, so they could both read them. She sipped her coffee as she scanned them.

"He and his wife Della had a daughter and a son," Simone said. "Their daughter never married and died five years ago from Amyotrophic Lateral Sclerosis or ALS."

"Oh, that's sad."

"Yes, it must have been hard, as a parent, to watch it happening. And Della never recovered from their daughter's death and passed away a year later."

"So he's been a widower for four years. What about his son?"

"It says here that Bert and his son, Dalton, have been estranged for three years." She read further. "It seems Dalton wanted to borrow some money to invest in an import/export business and Bert refused to lend it to him. They haven't spoken since."

"Money does cause a lot of problems in some families. So, basically he has no one in his life. No wonder he moved into Arbutus Hall. He must have been very lonely."

"Yes, and Mom is lonely, too." Simone picked up the papers and stuffed them back in the envelope. "I don't think we need to learn anymore."

"What about the two accounts."

Simone withdrew the papers again and looked them over. "It looks like Bert has one for his pension deposits and the other for his savings. It doesn't show the balances but Raymond wrote that they are healthy. Nothing sinister there."

"What's going on?"

Both women jumped at the sound of their mother's voice.

"Nothing." Simone shoved the papers in the envelope.

"I heard Bert's name." Patricia grabbed the envelope. "Are you two still checking up on him?" She pulled the papers out and looked at them. She gaped at her daughters. "You are. You ignored my wishes and hired that detective again."

"It's not as bad as it looks," Simone protested.

"Yes, we just wanted to know what happened to his wife and if he had children."

"You could have asked me or him. You didn't have to sneak around." Patricia tore the papers in half and threw them on the table. "You know, he really liked meeting you two and he is anxious to spend time getting to know you."

"You never said anything to us."

171

"I was going to when I told you that I invited him for dinner tomorrow night."

"We can get to know him then." Simone had that feeling again of being a child caught doing something wrong. That was twice since moving in with her mother. But this was worse than anything she'd done back then. She was eager to correct the mistake she and Serena had made. "I'd like to get to know him."

"Yes, I would also," Serena chimed in.

"You seem to know everything about him already, probably more than I do."

"We just know that his daughter died five years ago and his wife a year later," Simone said. "And he hasn't talked to his son for years."

"I heard you talking about his bank accounts. I can't believe you did that. I've told you he's not after my money."

"Yes, Mom," Serena said. "We know that."

"But my word wasn't good enough for you. You still had to check."

"We're sorry." Simone didn't know what else to say.

"You both better be. And I'm cancelling the dinner with Bert. I'm embarrassed to have him get to know my daughters after this. Now take me home."

"Yes, Mom." Simone scrambled from the booth and followed her mother out the door while Serena paid for their coffees.

The ride to Patricia's house was silent. Simone glanced at her mother a couple of times wanting to say something but Patricia's stony countenance kept her quiet. However, her curiosity finally got the better of her.

"How did you know we were there?"

"Like I've said before, you two would make poor criminals. I saw your car parked in front of it when I came out of Francine's house. Your red Mercedes is hard to miss."

"Oh." Simone felt so dumb. Obviously her mother was right about her and Serena and crime. They couldn't even fool their own mother.

"I actually thought you were waiting for me. I thought you might be planning to buy me coffee or lunch. Silly me."

Patricia's anger was palatable and Simone kept quiet the rest of the drive.

"You can go to your office now," Patricia said as she climbed out of the car.

Simone knew when she was being dismissed and she drove out of the yard. She didn't like the idea of leaving her mother alone but had no choice. She wouldn't be gone long.

* * *

Serena watched her sister and mother drive away glad she wasn't in that car. Poor Simone. Was she being yelled at or getting

173

the silent treatment? One was just as bad as the other.

She wondered how she and Simone could make it up to their mother. It would have to be something impressive, something that showed their love, something that would force her to forgive them. That something, though, she could not think of. Maybe Simone would come up with it.

Serena checked her cell for the time and realized she would just make her lunch with Albert. She had met him on *Meet and Match.com* and learned that he was a corporate lawyer. He lived in a large house with an ocean view in Delta.

Serena thought about Simone while she drove to Earl's Restaurant. How was she doing? Had Patricia calmed down or was she still mad? Was she yelling at Simone like she had when the girls were young and had done something wrong? Serena was glad to get to Earl's and pull into their lot. At least she would have a distraction for a little while.

She stepped out of her Prius and looked around. She saw a man wearing a Canucks cap standing beside his car just down the street. He had his phone in his hand. She waved and called to him. When he didn't see her she started towards him.

"Albert?"

"Jessica?" he asked.

Serena paused. What was going on? Did she have the wrong man? "Umm, no Serena."

"Oh, hi Serena. What a surprise to see you. I'm waiting for a woman named Jessica whom I've never met before."

"Then you may have sent me the text instead of her." Serena sighed inwardly. What a way to start a date.

He just stared at her.

"You sent me a text yesterday asking me if I wanted to meet you here at Earl's."

"Oh, I thought that was Jennifer." Albert waved his cell phone in the air. "This darn phone sometimes doesn't show me the names of the people I'm texting, so I get the conversations mixed up." He put it in his pocket. "But I'm glad it's you."

Nice try at saving the situation, Serena thought.

"Shall we go in?"

"Yes." Serena smiled. She was here already so might was well make the best of it and have lunch. Plus, a person never knew when she might need a lawyer.

Inside, they found a table and both asked for coffee when the server came over. Serena opened the menu. She wasn't really hungry and decided on a small bowl of clam chowder. Albert ordered a vegan street corn avocado dip with corn tortillas.

Serena had been texting with Albert but nothing important had been discussed, mainly the weather and the Canucks. Some sites offered a list of topics for first daters to discuss, but Serena couldn't remember any of the questions she should be asking. Apparently, Albert had paid more attention.

"So, have you lived in the Vancouver area all your life?"

"Yes. What about you?"

That seemed to be the opening he was waiting for. "I was born in Ireland and moved to Canada with my family when I was three. We lived in Ottawa, then Regina, and finally came to Vancouver when I was fourteen. My father is a lawyer and that's why I became one, too. He started his own firm twenty years ago and I joined it as a partner as soon as I was called to the British Columbia Bar. I've been a partner for twelve years. My dad is thinking of retiring and I'll be taking over his practice."

"How nice for you."

"Yes. My brother and sister are mad about it, but they had their chance to get into law with dad. He wanted all of us to be lawyers and join his practice so we would keep the firm going after he retired. He wanted his name to live on. They, instead, chose to do other things. My brother is a contractor and my sister is a veterinarian. They think my dad should sell me the firm and give them the money."

"Why?" Be a good listener was one of the suggestions on some of the dating sites. Another was don't hog the conversation. She doubted she would have any concern about that one.

"Because they both owe a lot of money. My brother was sued by a house builder because he scrimped on the cement for some basements and he lost in court, and my sister just bought a building to set up her own veterinary clinic."

Serena wasn't sure what Albert expected her to say to that, but she didn't have to worry. He carried right on to another subject recommended for first daters.

"Do you have any hobbies?"

"No. I'm pretty busy running my pub." Her phone pinged, but she ignored it. In spite of all the evidence of people sitting together at a restaurant table but talking on their cells or reading something on the screen, she still thought it was impolite to answer a cell phone when dining with someone.

"I have a complete miniature railway set up in my basement. It has over a kilometre of track, three villages, lakes, mountains, two engines, and fifteen cars. There are two separate tracks and the trains go in different directions."

"That sounds interesting." Serena was able to get a word in while the server set their food in front of them.

"It is. I made everything myself except for the railway cars and tracks. Those I bought from a miniature train store. I started collecting the cars when I was still a teenager and when I had enough to make a train, I built everything else. I bought sixteen four by eight sheets of plywood and built saw horses to hold them. Then I painted them and constructed the mountains and formed basins for the lakes from cement."

He paused to take a breath and Serena wondered if he was going to stop to eat. She had almost finished her soup.

"I built little houses and other structures for the villages and placed handmade train stations beside the track for the engines to stop at. I had to buy little people to stand on the platform waiting for the train. There are seats in the cars for the people to sit on when the train moves.

"There's so much that I can't describe," he finally stopped. "You'll have to see it in order to fully comprehend how much work I did. We could go after lunch."

Oh, god, no. "I really should get back to my pub." Serena took out her wallet to pay for her meal. "I've been gone all morning."

"That's too bad. There's so much we haven't talked about yet. We'll have to meet again."

"Yes, sometime." She wasn't going to tell him right now that she wasn't interested in him or his trains. She would slowly stop texting him, maybe ghost him.

Serena laid some money on the table. This was one of the reasons she liked to carry cash. She could pay and leave quickly.

"Goodbye," she said and didn't wait for a response. He was engrossed in eating his tortillas and dip.

Another great date under her belt, she thought ruefully, and another talk coming up with her bedpost.

* * *

Simone sat at her mother's kitchen table and scrolled through the real estate ads for condos and townhouses. She was getting discouraged. There were a lot of them for sale and the prices for most were way beyond her means. The ones she could afford were too far away for her to make the drive to her office each day.

She hadn't thought about finding a place just yet, thinking she could stay with her mother for a few months or at least until the condo sold and she had money to look for another place to live. But her mother's anger this morning had shown her that it would be better for her to move out. She and Serena had overstepped the bounds of being good daughters and, even though they had done it to protect their mother, they should have trusted her to know how to look after herself where men were concerned.

Then she had a thought. In spite of her earlier qualms about living in the condo with the memories of Griffin, maybe, she should buy him out. Maybe she should move back into their condo. She did like its location and she loved the view from the deck. And eventually those memories would fade, especially if she redecorated it. She felt an excitement growing in her as she did some figuring and decided she could handle the new monthly payments if she remortgaged it or took a second mortgage to pay him.

It would take Simone a month to get the bank paperwork done to have the condo put in her name. Then Griffin would move out and she back in. The redecorating could wait until summer. Candace was due to start on Monday and, if she worked out, Simone would see if Candace could move into Patricia's house in the New Year to look after her full time.

Simone felt a great relief. Her life was getting back on track. She sent a text to Griffin with her plan and said they would have to cancel the contract with the real estate agent. He replied immediately that he agreed to sell his half of the condo to her.

Simone smiled. Maybe things were starting to get better.

Patricia had entered the kitchen. She stopped when she saw Simone.

"Hi, Mom. What would you like for lunch?"

Patricia poured herself a coffee and left without saying a word. Simone sighed. She and Serena were in deep trouble and she didn't know how to fix it.

Her cell phone rang. She saw Unknown Caller and a phone number. She didn't recognize it and figured it was probably a telemarketer. She decided to let it go to voice mail.

She waited and when it dinged, she called voicemail to listen to the message. She fully expected someone to tell her that she had a package at customs or that her credit card had been used to make purchases in Florida. She was surprised to hear a man's voice saying he was Bert Madden.

"Your mother called me and cancelled our dinner tomorrow night. She told me about your investigation into my past. I'm so sorry you and your sister felt you had to check up on me. I guess I should have insisted on meeting you two a long time ago, so you could get to know me and see that I love your mother and would never do anything to hurt her. Would it be possible for you and Serena to have coffee with me this afternoon? Let me know."

Simone played it again, then she texted Serena.

Chapter Thirteen

Simone read over the contract, digitally signed the last page, and sent it back to the real estate agent. She and Griffin had now cancelled the sale of the condo. She was glad she had made that decision and that their real estate agent was so understanding. Saturday she would go to the bank and start the process of buying Griffin out and she would stop in to pick up her key from the real estate agent.

Simone's phone rang. She stood and headed up to her bedroom. She didn't want her mother to overhear the conversation.

"What do we do now?" Serena asked.

"I don't know." Simone shut her bedroom door. "This is getting out of hand."

"Yes. Do you think we should meet with him?"

"Mom will find out. She always does. And she will consider that we're going behind her back again. And we will be dragging Bert into her anger."

"We could do it over the phone." Serena suggested.

"Yes, then she won't find out unless he tells her. I'll phone and see if he's okay with that and get back to you."

"Okay."

Simone called the phone number and listened to it ring. If he didn't answer should she leave a message? She decided not. If her mother ever heard it...

"Hello?"

"Mr. Madden, this is Simone."

"Thank you for returning my call. Are we able to meet?"

"Would we be able to talk over the phone?" Simone didn't want to say that she was afraid of Patricia finding out about the meeting and being mad at all three of them.

"I'm old school. I'd much rather do this in person. It would be easier for us to really get to know each other face to face. Please, it's important to me."

"Okay. Where and when would work for you?"

"I believe Patricia has her line dancing this afternoon. We could meet after you drop her off."

Patricia hadn't said anything about Simone taking her to her dancing session. Maybe she had decided not to go, not wanting to have anything to do with Simone, who would be her ride there. Or maybe she was going by taxi.

"I'll check with Mom and see if she's going today. I'll phone you back."

Simone went downstairs and knocked on the closed office door. "Mom, may I come in?"

There was no answer. Simone tried again. Had something happened to her? She tried the knob and it turned. She slowly opened the door and peeked in. Patricia was at her desk typing on her computer. Had she not heard the knock or was she ignoring her?

"Mom."

Patricia kept typing, her face hard.

"Mom. Are you going line dancing this afternoon? I can take you."

Patricia stopped and looked up and her face softened. "I would like to go."

Simone breathed a quiet sigh. Maybe things would work out. "Where is it and what time do you have to be there?"

"It's at the seniors centre and I have to be there by two-forty-five."

Simone checked her watch. It was one thirty. "I'll make us some sandwiches and then we can leave."

Patricia nodded.

Simone hurried up to her bedroom and made her phone call to Bert. "I can meet you at three."

"Good. There's a restaurant a block away from the centre called Bonita's Kitchen. I'll meet you and Serena there."

Simone looked up the address and texted the information to Serena then added. *Bert wants to meet in person. He feels we can get to know each other better that way.*

184

I'll be there.

Simone made two ham, cheese, and mayo sandwiches. She carried a plate with a glass of orange juice to the office. She knocked and this time her mother called, "Come in."

Simone placed the plate and glass on the desk away from the computer. "Enjoy."

"Thank you."

Simone was a little disappointed that Patricia didn't say anything more. Little steps. She went back to the kitchen and ate her sandwich. She'd just put her plate in the dishwasher when her phone rang. Detective Small showed up on the screen with the phone number. She hesitated. It had to be something about Lauren.

"Hello."

"Ms. Bell. This is Detective Small of the Vancouver Police. I just want to let you know that we have arrested Ms. Lauren Huckley."

"Oh." Simone was surprised. She'd thought Lauren would have left the country. She would have been able to live for a long time in one of the South American countries on all the money she'd taken.

"She will have a bail hearing this afternoon in court or by telephone or video conferencing depending on how busy the courts are and she will probably be released."

"Does my mother have to be there?"

"No. We'll contact her when we need her. We also have Mrs. Bell's car. It will have to stay in our compound until the trial, if there is one."

"Do you think my mother might be in any danger from Ms. Huckley?" It felt funny to be calling Lauren by her last name. She'd been 'Lauren' for years.

"No. Part of her bail order will be that she doesn't have any contact with your mother. But your mother can also file a restraining order against Ms. Huckley if she wishes."

"Okay, thank you."

Simone decided she would tell Patricia about Lauren at dinner tonight. She didn't want to mention it to her until after she and Serena had spoken with Bert this afternoon. Maybe she would ask Serena here for dinner, so the three of them could discuss what to do.

"I'm ready," Patricia stood in the doorway, her coat and purse in hand. She handed Simone a piece of paper. "Here's the address."

"Let's go then." Simone smiled and picked up her own coat. She dug her keys out of her purse.

* * *

Serena checked the text messages on her burner phone on her way out to the car. One was from Albert wondering if she wanted to see his train set this weekend.

It's all set up for Christmas with decorated trees and lights on the houses. Very colourful.

"I don't think so," Serena muttered.

She returned her burner to her purse just as her cell phone binged. A text from Simone. Maybe an update on their mother's mood.

She read the text then read it again.

Lauren has been arrested. She appears in court this afternoon. Probably will get out on bail. Come for dinner tonight. We can tell Mom together and decide what to do.

That was a shock. She hadn't expected the police to do much in trying to find Lauren. After all, there were more serious crimes being committed in the city every day.

Has Mom forgiven us? Will she want to see me?

She let me make her lunch. I think if you show up with dinner she will be glad to see you.

Okay. I'll pick up Chinese food. Serena started her car and headed to Bonita's Kitchen. She spotted Simone's car parked on a side street. She smiled. Simone wasn't going to get caught by their mother again. She pulled in behind the Mercedes and climbed out.

Serena entered and looked around. The room had booths down each side and tables in the middle. The only Christmas decorations were a small tree in a far corner and a wreath hung on one wall. Jazz music played from the speakers. Not everyone got in the Christmas spirit.

Serena saw Simone and Bert sitting in a back booth. Another strategy not to be seen. She slid in beside Simone. They each had a menu in front of them and there was one at Serena's spot. "Hello, Bert," Serena said.

The server came over and they each asked for coffee. None of them wanted anything to eat so he removed the menus.

"First, I would like to thank you both for coming on such short notice," Bert said. "We don't have much time, so I will get right to the point. I know you are worried about your mother but please know that I love her very much. And I would never hurt her."

"We understand," Simone said. "And we're very sorry. It was never our intention to cause Mom and you so much trouble. She had never mentioned you and we were just so surprised at how advanced your relationship seemed to be."

"We had discussed telling you two about me and decided I would meet you at Christmas. We never thought there would be changes in her life before then."

"And Mom decided to make the introduction early and we screwed that up." Serena looked at Simone. "We just love her," She said, lamely.

"I understand. There are so many scams out there that we all have to be careful." Bert took a deep breath. "You know about my wife, my daughter, my son, and my two bank accounts, which each have over a million dollars, so I'll tell you a little about the rest of my life. I was born and raised in Ottawa. I got my optometrist license and moved here to practice. I met Della and we married and had Ginger and Dalton. I have one brother, Peter, and one sister, Marianne, both still living in Ottawa. Is there anything else you want to know?"

"No." Serena shook her head, embarrassed that they had thought this man might be after their mother's money and may even have had something to do with his wife's death. But she could understand why he had moved into Arbutus Hall, she thought. He must have been very lonely after his daughter and wife died and the fight with his son.

The server returned with their coffees and a bowl of cream containers.

"Do you have any relatives here in Vancouver?" Simone asked as she sipped her coffee.

"Dalton lives here. He's married with three children. I haven't seen them since our fight. After he quit speaking with me, he and his family moved to Ontario for a year. Della and I had spent our holidays there when Ginger and Dalton were young, so they could get to know my family. Marianne didn't have children and she doted on both of them. She and Dalton are still close, so she keeps me informed on how he's doing. He moved back here two years ago. According to her, the investment he wanted the money for turned out to be a pyramid scheme. He told her he's glad that I didn't let him have the money to invest. He's just opened his own accounting firm."

So she and Simone weren't the only ones who checked up on people. Bert had been keeping track of his son for three years.

Bert looked from one sister to the other. "I have a question for you."

Serena braced herself for the expected tirade of 'who did they think they were, investigating him?' or 'why didn't they ask him about his life instead of going behind his back?' But Bert reached in his pocket and pulled out a small box. He opened it and showed them a ring with an oval amethyst stone set in white gold.

"I had this made with your mother's birth month stone. I never thought I would find another woman to love as much as I love Patricia, so I'm asking both of you for permission to request your mother's hand in marriage."

Serena gasped. She hadn't been expecting this at all. She didn't know what to say.

He looked eagerly from one of them to the other.

"I think it's a wonderful idea," Simone said.

"Me, too," Serena echoed. "When do you plan on asking her?"

Bert beamed at them. "Tomorrow afternoon when you bring her to the hall. And if she agrees, I would like to get married before Christmas."

"That's not very far away," Serena said. "There's a lot of arrangements that have to be made.

"We're not getting any younger. Besides, it's not as if we have to plan a large wedding."

"We'll help you all we can," Simone said.

"Thank you." Bert put the ring back in his pocket. "And now I think Serena and I should get out of here and you should go pick your mother up."

"Yes, I told her I was going to do some shopping while I waited for her."

"Do you need a ride back to Arbutus Hall, Bert?" Serena asked, as they stood.

"If you don't mind. I decided not to drive my car here because of parking." He winked at Simone. "Plus, your mother knows what it looks like."

Simone laughed. "You're a lot smarter than me."

Serena walked with Bert to her vehicle and unlocked the doors. Arbutus Hall wasn't very far away and they soon arrived at the front door.

"It will be nice to have you in our family," Serena said.

"Thank you," Bert said, a catch in his voice. "It will be nice to have a family again." He climbed out of the Prius and waved as she pulled away.

Serena headed to the nearest Chinese food restaurant and ordered sweet and sour pork, beef and vegetables, chicken fried rice, noodles, and shrimp. While she waited, she thought about Bert and her mother and all the questions that went with Bert's proposal. Would Patricia say yes? Would she agree to a quickie wedding? Where would they live? Would Bert move into the house or would her mother move to Arbutus Hall? These were questions she had but only Patricia and Bert could answer them, for she was going keep out of it. She'd learned her lesson about meddling in her mother's affairs.

When her order was ready Serena drove to her mother's house. She hoped Simone was right that her bringing food would make her mother happy to see her.

* * *

"Mom, we have something to tell you," Simone said once they were seated at the table.

"Well, spit it out."

So they weren't off the hook yet where their mother was concerned. Good thing she didn't know about this afternoon.

"I received a phone call from Detective Small. He told me that Lauren has been arrested."

"They found her?" Patricia put down her fork. "Where was she? Is she going to jail?"

"She's probably out on bail right now. And according to what Detective Small said, she has to stay away from you."

"And that's what we want to talk with you about," Serena said. "We're not sure if we can trust her to stay away and we think you shouldn't be here. You should go away a few days, maybe come and stay with me."

"Why?" Patricia looked from one to the other.

"Well, we're not quite sure how Lauren will react to being arrested. She might be angry at us."

"She wouldn't hurt me, any of us." Patricia looked at them. "She wouldn't."

"I'm afraid we don't know that for sure." Simone put her hand on her mothers. "We never thought she would steal from you either."

"Oh, I really miss her." Patricia dabbed her eyes with her napkin. "I miss our outings, our games of backgammon, and the way she made lasagna."

"But all that time she was taking money from your account," Serena stressed.

"Maybe she had a good reason," Patricia said angrily. "Did you ever think of that? Maybe we should find out why she needed the money."

Serena looked at Simone. This wasn't going well. All they were accomplishing was upsetting their mother again. "Would you like another shrimp?" Serena picked up the container and handed it to Patricia.

Patricia waved it away with her hand. "I think I'm finished." She stood. "And I'm not going to your place, Serena. I'm staying in my home."

Serena watched her mother leave the room then turned back to Simone. "What do we do now?" She seemed to be asking that question a lot.

"Maybe if we give Mom time to think it over and she might realize we are right."

"I somehow doubt that. We know she was very attached to Lauren."

Serena leaned closer to Simone and whispered. "Do you think it's strange that Bert seems in a hurry to marry Mom?"

"A little, but we know that he has his own money. And like he said, they aren't getting any younger."

"I hope so and his proposal will certainly take Mom's mind off Lauren." Serena stood. "I'll help you clean up and then head back to my pub."

Chapter Fourteen

Simone was still in bed when she received a text from Bert.

Just confirming that I'm going to ask your mother to marry me this afternoon when you bring her. And that you and Serena will be here.

Simone smiled. It sounded like he might be getting a little nervous.

I'll come in when I drop Mom off and Serena will be there. Fingers crossed for you.

A thumbs up appeared.

Bert just checked to make sure that we will be at Arbutus Hall this afternoon at two. Simone sent Serena.

Serena texted back a ring, a cake, a Christmas tree, and a party emoji.

Simone showered and dressed and went downstairs. The kitchen was empty. She made a pot of coffee then found a box of dry cereal and poured herself a bowl. She added milk and sat at the island to eat it.

She wondered where her mother was. It was past ten and usually her mother would be on her second cup of coffee by now.

Maybe she was on a writing spurt and didn't want to stop. If that was true, it would be worth Simone's life if she disturbed her, even if it was to bring her a cup of coffee.

Simone looked at the clock on the wall. She still had time to read a couple of emails containing submissions. She returned to the bedroom and opened her computer. She brought up the next synopsis in her submission's file and read it. The story was about a mystery set on Vancouver Island during WWII. As she read it she felt a knot in her stomach. Wow, if the first three chapters delivered then she would want the full manuscript. She opened the attachment and it wasn't long before she was engrossed in the story.

When she was finished, she forwarded the email to Jilly and Romana. She hoped they would agree to her telling Grace to send a message to the author asking for the remainder of the manuscript.

The second synopsis wasn't as compelling but Simone opened the attachment and began reading. After the second page, she closed it and asked Grace to send this author a rejection letter.

She'd just opened the third email when there was a knock. "Come, in."

Patricia peaked around the door. "It's just about time for us to leave."

"It is?" Simone looked at the alarm clock on the night stand. One-thirty. "Oh, my. I didn't realize so much time had gone by. I'll be right down."

Simone ran a comb through her hair, applied lipstick and went downstairs. Patricia was sitting at the kitchen table, coat already on. Simone smiled. If she only knew what was in store for her this afternoon.

Simone and Patricia walked in the front door of the hall. Simone now wished she'd thought to ask how Bert planned on popping the question. Was he going to drop to one knee as soon as Patricia came in, or would he ask her while he and Patricia were in his room having sex, or did he plan on showing her the ring in the games room in front of all their friends and the staff? She helped her mother out of her coat and hung both of them up in the closet.

"What's Serena doing here?" Patricia asked as they walked into the common room.

"Serena?" Simone tried to sound surprised. "Where?"

"On the couch talking with Mona."

"Umm, I don't know." Simone looked around and noticed that the room was full of people who were pretending to ignore them. Four were playing pool while a crowd watched but it didn't seem as if the participants were being careful with their shots. Three tables had card players at them but everyone was just clutching their cards. Even the two ladies putting a puzzle together were just holding pieces in their hands. Everyone would surreptitiously look in

Patricia's direction and then away again. The room had an air of suspense in it. If Patricia noticed she didn't say anything.

"Hi, Patricia," Mona called. "I was just having a wonderful conversation with your daughter."

"Why are you here?" Patricia asked Serena.

"I'd thought I would come and play cards again with Mona and Adele. Plus, maybe we could visit with Bert awhile."

Simone wondered if Serena was that fast a thinker or if she'd rehearsed the answer in case it was needed.

"Patricia." Bert grinned as he walked into the room. Everyone fell quiet.

"Bert."

For the first time in days, Simone saw Patricia smile. She also noticed some of the staff hovering in the doorways and guessed the big event was about to happen.

Bert walked up to Patricia and took both her hands. He kissed her on the cheek then pulled the little box from his pants pocket. He slowly bent down on one knee.

"Bert?" Patricia gasped.

"Patricia we have known each other for only a few short months, but I have grown to love you very much and I want to spend the rest of my life with you." He opened the box to show her the engagement ring. "Will you marry me?"

There was an expectant hush in the room as everyone waited for Patricia to answer.

"I thought you'd never ask," Patricia said. "Yes, I will marry you."

The room erupted in clapping and cheering as Bert stood and removed the ring from the box. He slipped it on Patricia's finger and then hugged her tightly.

Simone looked at Serena and grinned. They were getting a stepdad.

Bert held up his hand for quiet. "I know it's usually the bride's task to make all the arrangements for her wedding including picking the day, but I want to get married before Christmas, and I hope she agrees with me." Bert stopped and looked at Patricia.

"Christmas is a week and a half away," Patricia protested.

"I know but I'm willing to help plan the big day. In fact I've already started by asking the management if we can hold it here and they've agreed."

"Oh, that would be lovely," Patricia agreed.

"And I've checked with a catering business and if we have the wedding on a Wednesday, they can cater it."

"You were pretty sure I would say yes," Patricia teased.

"I was definitely hoping."

"What else have you arranged?"

"I think we should be prepared for a lot of guests." Here Bert raised his voice, "because I want to invite everyone who lives and works here to attend."

Again, cheering and clapping filled the room and the residents and staff nodded and yelled that they would come.

Patricia smiled as she looked around the room. "Well, it seems my only job for this wedding is to find a dress and I think I can manage that by Wednesday."

"Circle December 20th on your calendars, everyone," Bert yelled. "There's going to be a wedding!"

Simone went up to her mother and gave her a hug. "Congratulations, Mom."

Serena put her arms around both of them. "Yes, Mom. I am so happy for you."

"Thank you. And we are going to have a chat about how you both just happened to be here for the big question."

Simone looked at Serena and grimaced. They were in trouble again.

* * *

Before Simone had taken Patricia back to her house Thursday afternoon, Bert and Patricia talked with the manager of Arbutus Hall about when would be the best time for the wedding and the luncheon afterwards, who of the staff and residents had food allergies, and if they could borrow the cutlery and plates. Bert phoned the caterer and said that they needed a lunch catered for this coming Wednesday. They agreed on the egg salad and cucumber sandwiches they had discussed and a regular white cake. He stated the number of residents and staff who would be attending plus he added another twenty for family and friends of the happy couple.

Simone had been impressed with how much planning he'd already done even before popping the question. Now, Friday afternoon, Simone, Patricia, and Serena were in Patricia's sitting at the dining room table composing a list of the few wedding arrangements left to be made before the wedding.

"We need flowers, napkins, table clothes, and centre pieces," Serena said as she wrote them down on the list.

"Bert and I have to get our license and find a Justice of the Peace."

Serena added them to the list.

"There isn't time to send out invitations so is there anyone you want to phone and invite, Mom?" Simone asked.

"Yes, a few. I'll do that tomorrow."

Simone noticed that Patricia hadn't said anything about best men or bridesmaids to stand up with them. Bert didn't have any male family in the city, except Dalton, but surely he had a friend or two he could ask. She and Serena had thought their mother would ask them to be her bridesmaids and when she didn't, they didn't bring up the subject. It was her decision.

"I need to go into my office and look at dresses on the Internet," Patricia said.

"Rather than us huddle around your desktop computer, I'll bring mine down." Simone stood and went upstairs. She returned quickly with her laptop. She set it on the table and they arranged their chairs around it.

Patricia typed in wedding dresses. "Hmmm, only 259,000,000 websites to choose from," she said dryly. She scrolled down the first page which showed young women in long white dresses with white veils and trains. "Well, these aren't what I'm looking for."

"What do you have in mind?" Serena asked.

"I don't really know except it's not going to be full length and there won't be a veil or train."

"Do you want a white one or a colour one?"

"Some sort of colour. I'm too old to claim I'm a virgin."

"What if we bring up dress shops in Vancouver?" Simone asked.

Patricia did and then clicked on "10 Best Dress Shops in Vancouver". She went down the list and opened each site but all they showed were reviews and hours and location. None of them showed dresses for them to view.

They tried a few more sites and most of them showed young, skinny women in long dresses suitable for a red carpet walk.

"This is why I like to go shopping in person," Patricia said. "I can walk up and down the aisles looking at dresses, take any I like off the rack, check the colour under the store lights and sunlight, and try them on. You can't do that on a computer."

"I have to go to the bank tomorrow to arrange a second mortgage on the condo so I can buy Griffin out. You can come with me and we can go looking at dresses afterward." She didn't want Patricia to be at home in case Lauren came for a visit.

"I'll come, too," Serena said. "I need a new dress for the wedding."

"You're going to wear a dress?" Patricia asked surprised. "I haven't seen you in anything except pants since you were in the beauty pageants."

"I have a few in my closet," Serena protested. "It's just that I don't go many places where dressing up is required. And jeans are more comfortable."

"Well, thank you for making the sacrifice for me," Patricia smiled.

Simone was glad to see that the wedding arrangements had taken her mother's mind off her and Serena's nosiness. While it had sounded as if they were in trouble yesterday, Patricia's happiness and excitement had calmed her anger and when they told her that Bert had asked their permission to marry her, she'd been touched by his old-fashioned approach.

"My pleasure." Serena did a slight curtsy.

"And what about you, Simone? What do you plan on wearing to my wedding?"

"I was waiting for you to pick your dress before buying one for myself. I don't want us to clash."

"Good. So all three of us will buy our dresses at the same time. I would like yours to be similar in colour because I would like you both to walk me down the aisle or whatever it is we're going to have me walk down."

"I would love to, Mom!" Serena flung her arms around her mother.

"Oh, Mom, I would be happy to," Simone said enthusiastically. She joined Serena in hugging Patricia. That answered why she hadn't asked them to be bridesmaids.

"What time should I come over tomorrow?" Serena asked.

"Well, Candace will be here from nine until noon, so I would say about one."

"Oh, in the excitement, I'd forgotten about her," Patricia said.

"Yes, she'd slipped my mind also," Serena admitted. "And now that we have most of the wedding day decided, there is just one last question. Do you know where you two will be living?"

"Oh," Patricia looked surprised. "I haven't even thought about it. This has been so sudden that Bert and I haven't had time to discuss it. I'll have to phone him and ask, but I expect he'll be moving in with me."

So, Simone thought, I'll have to find a place to stay before the wedding because it would be a while before the paperwork was done and Griffin moved out of the condo. One alternative was for her to move back in while Griffin was still there. She shuddered and decided that wasn't an option. Another one was for her to stay here. A second shudder. She didn't need to have her mom jump out of a closet at her thinking she was Bert.

She'd have to come up with a different plan and fast.

"Let's go to the Vancouver Christmas Market," Serena said. "I'm hungry and could eat a Bratwurst on a bun or some of their pretzels."

"And it's been a year since I've had a Hungarian flatbread with garlic spread," Patricia said.

"Yes, get that desire for garlic out of your system before getting married," Simone laughed as she put on her coat.

"I'll check to see if we can get tickets to it." Serena took out her cell phone and brought up the market. She went to tickets then admission and pricing. She clicked on Buy Now and brought up today's date. "The three of us can get in in an hour." She looked at the others. "Is that okay?"

"Yes," Patricia said.

Simone nodded.

Serena clicked on buy and purchased three tickets. She immediately received a reply with her tickets attached.

"We're good to go and we'll take my vehicle to save on parking," Serena said.

They loaded into Serena's Prius, drove to the parkade of the Vancouver Trade and Convention Centre, and paid at the pay machine.

"There," Serena said. "We have two hours."

They walked out to the West Waterfront Road in the growing dusk and to the Jack Poole Plaza. Serena showed their tickets before they joined the crowd inside. There were little wooden huts laid out like a Bavarian village with streets going in different directions.

"Did you know there are about eighty vendors here this year?" Patricia asked.

"Well, it's a popular venue," Serena said. "I come here every year."

They saw the hut with the pretzels and Serena bought a bag of them. The next stop was for Patricia's flatbread. Instead of the garlic spread, she asked for grated cheese and bacon bits. Simone decided on German-style Hurricane potatoes at Das Kartoffelhaus. She liked the deep fried, crunchy, spiralled-cut potato on a long skewer.

The huts were all lit up with multi-coloured lights, holiday music blared from speakers, and Christmas decorations hung everywhere. They ate their goodies as they wandered past the Olympic Cauldron which was lit up for the holidays and up and down the short streets of the village. They looked at the Christmas gifts and stocking stuffers, sampled some of the liquor, and stepped inside the giant Christmas tree and looked up at the thousands of sparkling lights.

Simone bought a one-of-a-kind necklace with matching earrings for Grace and each of her agents, while Patricia purchased some hand-dipped candles for her friends. As the early evening grew cooler, they bought hot apple cider. They wrapped their hands around the warm paper cups as they continued their tour.

A few minutes later, Serena looked at her cell phone. "We've got fifteen minutes until our parking time is up. I can go add more time if you want to stay longer."

"No, I've seen enough," Patricia said.

"Me, too," Simone echoed.

"Okay, let's go."

Chapter Fifteen

Simone smiled as she saw Griffin walking towards her. This time he was dressed more flamboyantly in a paisley shirt under a light purple jacket. His slacks were a darker purple and his shoes black. He had studs in his newly pierced ears.

Griffin grinned and hugged her. Simone readily returned it. She had come to terms with her feelings for him and that she was willing to get on with her life. This visit to the bank was a big step in moving that forward.

They went inside to their appointment with the mortgage specialist. Simone explained their plans and the specialist had them fill out the appropriate paperwork. Simone then gave Griffin a down payment cheque from her business account. She would return the money once the mortgage was in place. They decided that January first as the total possession date.

"I know New Year's Day is when I have to be out," Griffin said on their way out of the bank, "but I'm transferring my studies to a college in Kamloops, so I'll be moving there tomorrow. You can move back in anytime you want."

"Oh, that would be great." Her worries about a place to stay were over. And, if for some reason Bert didn't move in immediately, she could stay with her mother until he did.

"The place I'm moving into is furnished, so I'll be leaving the bedroom set also."

"Okay."

"Do you have time for a drink?" Griffin asked. "It will probably be the last time we see each other."

Simone checked her cell phone. Candace had shown up this morning and Patricia had walked her through the house explaining what she wanted done in the way of housework. Simone had noticed that Candace listened attentively to everything Patricia said and nodded in understanding. Then Candace had done the work exactly as Patricia wanted. She'd also prepared a light lunch for Patricia and Simone. Simone was happy. It looked as if they'd chosen the right woman.

Patricia had phoned Bert and they'd agreed that he would come over on Sunday so they could discuss where they would live after they married.

Then while Simone met Griffin, Serena took Patricia to a party place to buy napkins, tablecloths, and centre pieces. They'd agreed to meet at the first dress shop on their list at two-thirty. It was two-fifteen now and she still had to pick up her key at the real estate agency.

"Sorry, I can't. I have other plans." She doubted that he would be interested to know that her mother was getting married and they were going dress shopping.

"Okay," Griffin smiled. "Good luck in your future."

"And you, too."

Simone watched him walk away and felt a tug at her heart. She would definitely miss him in her life. She took a deep breath. Their life together was definitely over and nothing would change that. She went to her car and drove to the real estate office, picked up her key and headed to the dress shop. She hurried in to find her mother standing in front of a mirror in a light silver dress that reached to her knees. It was sleeveless with a short jacket.

"What do you think, Simone?" Patricia asked, twirling around.

"It is pretty," Simone replied somewhat reluctantly.

"But?"

"It seems to wash your colour out." She glanced at Serena for help.

"That's what Serena said," Patricia sighed. She turned to the saleslady. "This is my other daughter Simone. Simone, our saleslady, Ava."

Simone and Ava smiled at each other.

"I guess I'll try another one," Patricia said.

Ava followed Patricia to a rack of clothes. They pushed the hangers aside as they discussed each dress and checked the sizes.

"How did it go with Griffin?" Serena asked.

"Better than I expected. He's moving to Kamloops, so I'll be able to get my furniture out of storage and move into my condo before Bert moves in with mom."

"What do you think of this one?"

The sisters looked up and both went, "Wow."

Their mother stood before them in a gray, A-line dress that reached her shins. It was sleeveless chiffon with a V-neck. The long-sleeved, lace jacket totally covered it and a silver clasp held it closed at her waist.

"That's beautiful," Simone said.

"It fits you perfectly," Serena added. "I like the length."

"It's called tea-length," Ava said.

"What is that colour?" Simone asked.

"Stormy. It's been very popular with mothers of the brides."

"Oh, neither of us is getting married," Serena laughed. "Mom is the bride."

"Oh, congratulations," Ava gushed.

"Thank you and I'll take this one. Now to find dresses for my daughters."

"What colour do you have in mind, and do you want us to have the same style?" Simone asked.

"I think we should go with what suits each of you and if it's one you like. After all, they will be hanging in your closets."

While Patricia changed back into her clothes Simone and Serena started their search through the racks and racks of dresses. They spent the next hour trying many on, sometimes laughing at the look and other times just shaking their heads.

The three finally settled on light blue, tunic-style wrap dress for Simone with an hourglass shape, pockets, and a kimono belt. Serena's was a dusty blue, cowl neck, midi slip dress with spaghetti straps.

They paid for their dresses and left the shop. It was already getting dark and was raining.

"What do we want for dinner tonight?" Serena asked.

"Oh, something light," Patricia stated. "I'm so tired of the heavy restaurant food we've been eating lately."

"The Fresh Salad Bar has soups, salads, and fresh sliced fruit," Simone said. "I'll stop in on my way to Mom's."

Before going to the salad bar Simone drove to a department store and bought a burner phone. She had the sales person set up a phone number and pin number and put it in her purse. She liked the look and profile of some of the men on the dating site and thought she would like to contact some of them.

* * *

Serena left after they'd eaten and Patricia went to her office. Simone cleaned up the kitchen then brought up the dating site on her cell phone. She sent a message to three men. Now she just had to wait to see if any of them was interested.

Simone heard another phone ring. She looked around for where the sound was coming from. Patricia's cell was in a pouch on the outside of her purse on the counter. Simone pulled the phone out and hurried to the office. She knocked and then entered without waiting for summons.

"Your phone is ringing." Simone handed it to her.

"Hello."

Simone turned back towards the door.

"Lauren."

Simone stopped. She stared at Patricia.

"Yes, I'm willing to see you."

Simone waved her hands and shook her head. "No," she hissed. "You can't see her."

"Sure, you can come over tonight. We've changed the locks, so you will have to ring the bell." Patricia hung up.

"Mom, what are you doing?" Simone demanded. "She's not supposed to be contacting you. You can't see her."

"She said she wanted to come over and explain everything to me."

"What kind of an explanation is there for stealing eighty thousand dollars?"

"That's what we're going to find out, isn't it."

The doorbell rang.

Simone looked at her mother.

Patricia shrugged. "I don't know."

Simone went to the door, her mother following. She peeked out one of the side windows. Lauren stood beneath the light on the porch. Simone could see her breath in the cold air. Big flakes of snow were coming down.

"She's here."

"Well, let her in."

"Mom, I don't think this is a good idea."

Patricia impatiently waved her hand. She unbolted the lock and opened the door. She beckoned Lauren in. "Come in before you freeze. How did you get here so fast?"

"I was down the block when I phoned." Lauren stepped in. "I was just going to knock, but then I thought I'd better make sure it was okay to come."

"You know you're supposed to stay away from Mom," Simone said.

"Yes, and if you want me to go, I will."

"No, no," Patricia said. "It's okay. Come into the living room and sit down."

Lauren sat on one of the chairs and Simone and Patricia sat side by side on the couch.

"First of all, I am so sorry for taking the money."

"I'm sorry you took it, too. Why didn't you ask me for it? I would have loaned you some."

"I tried a couple of times but just didn't have the nerve. I figured it would be awkward for me to stay if you turned me down and I liked working for you. I just needed the money and didn't know what else to do."

"What was so important that you would steal that much money from a senior citizen?" Simone couldn't keep the anger from her voice.

Lauren looked down at her hands then up at Simone and Patricia. "It's a story that many families are facing these days. My sister, Wanda, has two children, that is, had two children. A girl named Kyra and a boy, Gregory. They were good kids and very close until Gregory experimented with heroin at a party when he was sixteen and got hooked almost immediately. Over the next two years, he sold everything he owned like his skateboard and bicycle to pay for his drugs. When that was gone, he pawned Wanda's late husband's power tools and scrap metal from the garage. He was arrested for burglary and quit school. He was let off with a fine, which Wanda paid, but he hadn't learned his lesson. He stole some of Wanda's jewellery and other things from around the house and sold them. Wanda tried to help him by paying for him to go into treatment but he never stayed long enough. When she caught him stealing money from her purse she finally kicked him out of the house.

"Kyra took that very hard and would search the streets for him to make sure he was okay. She had a job and gave him money for food, but by then he was selling drugs to earn money for his own. He overdosed twice and was saved by the EMT's giving him Naloxone. They couldn't save him the third time."

"Oh, I'm so sorry," Patricia said.

"Thank you, but that was before I began working for you and Craig."

"So that doesn't explain why you needed the money?" Simone said.

"Kyra had graduated high school and started university but losing her brother sent her into a depression. She began partying with a bad crowd. Soon she was into drugs and quit university. She went down the same path as Gregory and lived on the streets for a while. Wanda didn't have the money to get her into treatment, so that was when I began taking a little cash each month from your account. As soon as I had enough money, Wanda found a place for Kyra to go. She stayed the full three months and it looked as if she was going to get her life together but she was back on drugs within a month of leaving the place. So we tried again, this time finding a ranch where Kyra had to help look after the horses and other animals. It was very expensive but she seemed happy there and decided to stay longer after her three months were up. The only way we could pay for that was for me to continue taking money from you."

"So why did you leave here?" Patricia asked. "I never suspected anything."

Lauren looked at Simone. "When Simone moved in, I figured she might start checking up on things around here and find out."

"How is your niece now?"

Lauren smiled for the first time. "She's doing well. She's decided to go back to university next semester to become a psychologist. She wants to work with teenagers to try to keep them away from drugs."

They sat in silence for a few moments. Lauren cleared her throat. "I do have ten thousand dollars to give back to you. As soon as my trial is over and I get a job, I can start making payments."

"I'll take the money but use your earnings to help Kyra with her schooling," Patricia said, standing. "I'm happy you told me why you did it and I'm glad it worked out for her."

"Thank you." Lauren got up. "I'll send you a cheque."

"I'll phone the police tomorrow and drop the charges and get my car back." Patricia led the way to the door.

Simone followed the women. For a few minutes, she'd been afraid Lauren would ask for her job back and Patricia would give it to her. But it was clear that as much as her mother missed Lauren, she wasn't about to forgive her behaviour.

The snow was still coming down when Lauren left.

Before going to bed, Simone phoned Serena to tell her about Lauren.

"I'm still angry at the gall of that woman even if she had a good sob story," Serena said. "And I'm glad mom is getting some money back, although I don't like her decision to drop the charges."

"Me, too. But that's Mom's choice. At least she didn't ask Lauren to come back."

"Probably a good thing she'd already hired Candace."

Chapter Sixteen

After a breakfast of bacon and eggs with Patricia Sunday morning, Simone phoned the storage company and told the receptionist she would be cancelling her unit early.

"We don't do refunds."

"I understand."

Then she called the moving company and booked a truck and movers for the next day. She wanted to go check the condo today and do any necessary cleaning. Griffin hadn't helped much around their home, so she didn't know what to expect. Mind you, she hadn't left him much that would get dirty.

She went to her mother's office to ask what time Bert would arrive, but Patricia wasn't there. She looked in the other rooms and wondered if maybe she'd gone to her bedroom. Then she heard a noise outside.

She looked out the kitchen window and saw her mother with her coat on. She held a Himalayan salt shaker out in front of her and was twisting the top. What was going on now? Simone opened the door.

"Mom, what are you doing?"

"The cold froze the rain yesterday and then it snowed overtop. I shovelled off the heavy, wet snow but I couldn't find any ice melter salt in the garage or shed. Bert is coming, so I have to use this salt on the ice on the steps so he doesn't slip." Patricia dug in her coat pocket and pulled out two other salt shakers. "Take these and help me."

"I'll get my coat and boots on."

Simone stepped out in a few minutes and took the shakers. She felt a little silly shaking the table salt on the ice and was glad no one could see her. She doubted it would do much good anyway. When the shakers were empty, Simone and Patricia went back in the house.

"I'll text Bert and tell him to be careful when he comes."

Simone went to her bedroom and stretched out on her bed. She brought up a book submission on her computer. It was time to get to work.

An hour later she heard the doorbell ring. Bert had arrived as promised and survived the ice. Maybe the table salt had worked. She decided to stay where she was and let Patricia and Bert have time to discuss their living arrangements. She heard some giggling and laughing as she declined the submission then stood and stretched. It would have been nice to have a desk to work at, but she wouldn't be here much longer. She climbed back onto the bed and opened another.

Simone was half way through reading the first three chapters when there was a knock at her door.

"Simone?"

"Come in, Mom." Simone minimized the manuscript and closed her computer. "Hello, Bert," she said when they opened the door.

"I'm showing Bert the house. May he look in here?"

"Sure."

Bert peeked in the ensuite and opened the door of the walk in closet. He looked out the window.

"You girls had a lovely home to grow up in," Bert said.

"Yes, we were lucky."

"Thank you for letting me in." Bert turned to Patricia. "I guess it's time we had a serious discussion. Let's go for lunch and talk."

"See you later," Patricia smiled at Simone while Bert waved.

Simone wondered what they would decide. She shrugged. She would just have to wait. In the meantime, she had to go check on her condo.

It felt good to drive into the parking lot under her condo complex and park in her spot. It was hard to believe that mere days ago she'd moved out. So much had happened in those few days.

Simone let herself into the condo. It was so very quiet and her footsteps echoed as she walked through her home. Griffin had either cleaned the place or hadn't made much of a mess in the past thirteen days. The spare bedroom furniture was there as promised. It was going to be easy for her to move back in.

On the counter, she found Griffin's key and a bottle of their favourite wine. One of the things they'd discovered about each other on their first date was that they liked the same wine. It was expensive, so they only bought it on special occasions like their anniversary or Christmas or their birthdays. She decided to save it for when the divorce papers were officially signed, which would be in about a year. That would be the last special occasion she had with Griffin.

Simone opened the refrigerator door. It was empty and clean. She would have to go shopping on Monday after her furniture arrived.

She smiled as she locked the door and left the building. Back at her mother's, Simone made herself a sandwich and carried the plate up to her bedroom. She still had work to do on her computer.

Fifteen minutes later her burner phone dinged with a text. Simone picked it up and clicked on the message.

I see on your profile that you are a literary agent. I have written a great manuscript that you really need to read. It is along the lines of Dan Brown's books, but so much better written and exciting. We should meet, so I can give you the full manuscript and we can discuss it. You might want to bring along a contract because once you've heard the story line you'll realize it's the best manuscript you've received all year.

"Really?" Simone muttered. "That's your opening line. That's what's supposed to make me want to meet you?"

As per my website, you can send a synopsis and first three chapters. If I like it I will contact you for the rest of your manuscript. Might as well get rid of this guy fast.

Her cell phone pinged. Serena.

Anything yet?

Mom took Bert on a tour of the house and now they've gone for lunch and a talk. Will let you know if there's any news when they get back.

Simone took the plate down to the kitchen and poured herself a glass of water. The door opened and her mother and Bert came laughing into the house. Simone was glad to see her mother so happy. It had been a while since she'd heard the peals of Patricia's laughter in the house, definitely not since she'd moved in.

"Hi, Dear," Patricia said, taking off her coat.

"Sounds like you two had fun."

"We did and we made a lot of decisions."

"Oh?"

"I'll go back to the hall while you tell your daughter," Bert said. He smiled at Simone. "I hope you're okay with them."

Simone was surprised. Their decisions had nothing to do with her. "Whatever you two decide is good with me and I'll help you all I can."

"Thank you." Bert kissed Patricia, waved to Simone, and was gone.

"Do you want a sandwich or cup of tea?" Simone asked.

"No, we just ate." Patricia sat at the island.

"So, what's happening?" Simone joined her.

"Well, first of all, we went to the police station and I now have my car back. You don't need to chauffeur me around anymore. And Bert will be moving in here."

"That's good. I was wondering what you would do with this house if you moved."

"That was our biggest question. We decided that with help, we could live here for many years yet. He's already wanting to put in a vegetable garden beside my flowers and update the patio and buy a new barbeque. We haven't had a barbeque since your father died."

"Yes, Dad could really cook a steak."

"And he wants to buy a smoker. He misses being able to smoke brisket and salmon."

"Sounds like he's got a lot of plans."

"Yes, he says he needs something to do while I'm writing. And we want to travel. We're thinking of Mexico for our honeymoon."

Simone grinned. "All those plans in such a short time today."

"We don't have time to waste."

"Well, I'll be moving my furniture out of storage and into my condo tomorrow but will stay here until you two are married. Then my room will be free for company or to be turned into a she shed or a man cave."

"More likely it will be for company. Bert's hoping some of his family from Ontario will come and visit us. But I have to get back to the final edit of my manuscript. My agent is asking where it is."

Simone sent Serena a text with the outline of their mother's and Bert's plans for after marriage. *She also has her car back.*

I'm glad for Mom.

Yes, she has her spark and vitality back.

* * *

Serena put her phone away and went into the kitchen for the plates of food for one of the tables she was serving. It was nice to know that her life would soon be back to normal. Simone would be in her condo and their mom would be married and happily living with her new husband in her house, all before Christmas. She wondered if either of them had thought about where they would be meeting Christmas morning or who would be cooking Christmas dinner. She certainly hadn't.

Also, how did Bert celebrate Christmas? She didn't even know his religion. Not that it mattered. That was her mother's department.

Serena set the plates down in front of the customers and asked if any of them wanted freshly milled pepper. They all shook their heads.

"Enjoy you meal." Serena walked to the next table and picked up the empty plates. "Would you liked the dessert menu?"

"I'd like to see it again," one of the women said.

Serena took the dirty dishes to the kitchen then went to the podium at the hostess station and picked up four dessert menus. She placed them on the table. "I'll give you a few minutes."

A couple walked in and Noah greeted them with a smile. That was one thing she'd insisted upon when hiring any staff. They had to be friendly, outgoing, patient, and they had to remember the specials. They were allowed to eat one meal a day, so they could make recommendations from personal experience.

When the rush was over, Serena went to her office. She had paperwork to catch up on. Her cell and burner phones were both on her desk. That was another of her rules, no one, not even her, carried their cell phone with them when working. They could check for messages on their breaks.

There was a text on her burner from Steven, one of the men she'd only been texting for the past couple of days. He was accepting her invitation to a hockey game tonight. She seldom went to hockey games, but had bid on the tickets at a fund raiser in October and won. With what was happening with her sister and mother over the past week and a half, she'd forgotten about them until that morning.

She was breaking her own self-imposed rule about dating. Not to meet until after at least two weeks of texting. But she'd been striking out on the men she met after texting that long and she thought she'd try something different.

Meet you at the main entrance at six-fifteen. She sent back.

I'll be the one in a Canucks jersey.

Serena smiled. At least, he had a sense of humour.

The afternoon passed by fast and Serena left her office at five. She checked to make sure everything was running smoothly in the kitchen and front area then went to her condo. She wanted to get ready for the game. The text from Doug about wearing something classier when going out had rankled her. She decided that, since she didn't have a Canucks jersey to wear, she would dress up for the game. Not in a dress and heels kind of dress up, but more like skinny black jeans, black sweater, dangly zirconia earrings and matching large multilayered zirconia necklace, and her red wrap coat with belt and faux fur collar. Steven wouldn't be able to say she and her wardrobe needed improvement.

The Costco across from the arena allowed parking during events and Serena hoped she could find a spot there. She drove around and finally found one near the back. She paid her event fee price and walked to the main entrance of Rogers Arena. The sidewalk was a sea of blue and green jerseys, hoodies, and jackets. Many of the men and some of the women wore blue caps with green bills. Serena looked around helplessly. How was she going to find a guy in a Canucks jersey amongst these hundreds of men wearing jerseys?

"Serena?" a male voice tentatively asked.

"Yes." Serena turned around. It was a good thing he recognized her, because she would never have spotted him in the crowd.

"Nice to meet you," Steven said.

"You, too." Serena took the tickets from her purse and gave one to Steven. They got in line at the doors and once through, headed upstairs.

"Would you like a drink?" Steven asked.

"A glass of white wine, please,"

Steven went to the nearest bar and soon came back with a plastic glass of wine for her and one of beer for him. They went to their seats.

"Not much of a Canucks fan?" Steven asked.

"I'm more into football. I prefer to enjoy the fresh air when I watch the B.C. Lions."

"I guess my next question is why the tickets then and why did you invite me, since we've just connected."

"Good question. I was at a charity event and bid on these tickets. I'd forgotten about them until this morning. You mentioned in your profile that you were a Canucks fan, so I thought you might be interested in going."

"Well, your invite did take me by surprise and I do appreciate it."

The two teams come out on the ice and began skating around to warm up. The fans cheered as the puck was dropped and the game began. Serena tried a couple of times to find out more about Steven, but he was glued to the game. So she found herself looking around the arena, taking in the private suites, the hawkers walking up and down the stairs selling beer or popcorn, and the team mascot, Fin the Whale, beating his drum in different sections.

Steven jumped up along with most of the crowd in loud cheering.

Serena looked at the replay on the Jumbotron and saw that the Canucks had scored the first goal of the game and it was only the five minute mark. She sighed. This was going to be a long, painful night. Why hadn't she just given the tickets away?

During the break between the first and second period they walked around the causeway past people selling 50/50 tickets, merchandise stores, and food vendors. There were a lot of people like her who were in everyday clothes. Not everyone was wearing a jersey. They chatted a bit about each other's jobs, he was a computer expert/salesman in an electronics store. She told him she owned a pub.

"I'm going to get something to eat," Steven said. "Do you want anything?"

"No, thank you."

Serena waited while he got in line and was finally served. He came back with a hot dog loaded with onions, mustard, and ketchup. There was no more conversation as the second period began just as he finished his hot dog.

The Canucks scored once and the LA Kings scored twice to tie the game. They did another round of the causeway and then watched the last period in which the Canucks scored with two minutes left. The crowd was ecstatic. Steven was grinning ear to ear and high fiving the people around him. When the game ended, they worked their way through the happy crowd to the main entrance.

"I'd invite you for a drink," Steven said when they were out on the sidewalk again, "but I have to get up for work in the morning."

"Yes, me too." Serena was just as happy not to go. It had been a long, boring evening for her, even if not for him.

"Thank you for the game tonight. If I could make a suggestion, you might want to invest in a Canucks jersey. And the next time you go to a game, you should lose the bling and wear more appropriate clothing such as sweat pants and the jersey."

Serena stared at Steven's back as he hurried away through the crowd. Of all the nerve!

Then she laughed. Did all men think they had to tell a woman how to dress or was she just lucky enough to find them?

Chapter Seventeen

Simone rose early Monday morning and packed many of her clothes into the same garbage bags she'd brought them in. She left her new dress for the wedding and a couple of pairs of slacks and blouses. She carried the bags downstairs and threw them into her car. Patricia was in her office with the door closed. Simone left her a note then drove to her condo. The movers would be there at ten and she wanted to make sure she was there before them.

Serena arrived just in time to help her carry the bags upstairs. They talked while Simone hung up her clothes.

Serena told her about her date with Steven and his advice about how she dressed.

"Really?" Simone asked hanging up a black pantsuit.

"Yes, really. I'm supposed to buy a Canucks jersey if I decide to go to another game."

"Maybe he gets a commission," Simone grinned.

"Well, not this time."

"That's as bad as the guy who wanted me to meet him so he could give me a copy of the greatest manuscript ever written."

"And...?"

"I said sure."

"You what?"

"Just kidding. I told him to send the first three chapters to my agency email on my website."

"Well, at least you've started into the shadowy world of online dating. The further you go the darker it gets and the weirder your dates are. It's become a challenge for me to try and find a regular, nice guy. And I'm going to keep at it until I do. Because I've heard via the grapevine that there are such guys out there."

"Well, if Doug comes today you could try again with him. Maybe he's realized the error of his ways and will love you in spite of what you wear."

Serena stuck out her tongue. "I doubt it."

Simone's phone rang. It was the movers and they were downstairs. She buzzed them in and went to the elevator to wait for them. When the elevator doors opened, it was the reversal of her moving out day. They brought in the furniture and Simone showed them were to place it. Serena unpacked the boxes and put the dishes in the cupboards. By the end of the day Simone's condo was back to normal. The only thing missing were Christmas decorations. They were adorning her mother's house. She could bring her tree and set it up, though.

"Well, that went almost as fast as when I moved out," Simone said, flopping down on the couch after the movers left. "The only difference was Doug wasn't here to slip you his number."

"Ah, but Justin did." Serena waved a piece of paper as she sat on the overstuffed chair.

"Ah, the beauty and brains sister strikes again."

"And now this sister has to get back to work. I'll be at Mom's tomorrow night for the rehearsal."

After Serena left, Simone made up her bed and, as a precaution, stripped the guest bed to wash the sheets and pillow cases. She went through the cupboards and reorganized some of the dishes, pots, and pans. Once the bedding was in the dryer, she headed for the nearest grocery store and stocked up on the necessities like fruits, vegetables, meat, bread, butter, milk, eggs, and coffee, and non-necessities like muffins, Christmas cake, and chocolates. Once she was back for good, she would do a thorough shop for baking supplies and cleaning materials.

It was dark when Simone pulled into her mother's driveway. She entered the house to the smell of meatloaf. Ah, Candace was there this morning and made them dinner.

The office door stood open, so Simone went to lean in the doorway.

Patricia looked up and smiled. "Did you get all settled?"

"Yes, and I even got some shopping done."

Patricia stood. "Tonight we find out just how good a cook Candace is."

They walked back to the kitchen and Simone set the counter of the island. Patricia put the meatloaf on the counter along with two baked potatoes and a salad.

"Bert brought some of his clothes over today," Patricia said as they ate their meal. "His rent is paid to the end of the month, so he will take his time moving his other things. He might just sell his bedroom furniture since I have enough beds and dressers here."

"How are things going with the wedding plans?"

"Everything is in place. We have our license. Bert found a Justice of the Peace and asked one of his friends at the hall, Daniel, to be his best man and I choose my friend, June, as my Maid of Honour."

"Serena helped me unpack today and she said she would be here for the rehearsal tomorrow night. Is everyone else coming?"

"Yes, Bert, Daniel, and June. Candace plans to stay and cook the rehearsal meal."

"So everything is covered."

"I hope so."

* * *

Serena showed up early Wednesday morning dressed in her dusty blue dress. The wedding was at eleven with the lunch at twelve. Tuesday had been a whirlwind of getting the napkins, tablecloths, and centre pieces to the hall, deciding how the tables would be spaced, where the makeshift aisle would be, and where the JP would stand. One of the residents, who had operated a photo lab and camera shop before digital cameras became the rage, was going to take the pictures. And then Patricia's quick dash to the hairdresser to get her hair styled, and the rehearsal and dinner in the evening.

Serena was impressed with how her mother was holding up. With all the organizing and running around she and Bert had done the past few days, she still looked calm as Serena and Simone helped her dress.

"Do you know if Bert invited Dalton to the wedding?" Serena asked, as she fitted the small tiara in Patricia's hair.

"He didn't and that's too bad. Asking his son to be his best man would have been a great way for them to reconcile."

"It's funny to think that we're going to have a brother, well a stepbrother, and we may never meet him."

"Well, that might change once we're married. You know I like a happy ever after ending."

Simone carried four bouquets while Serena helped her mother out the door. They had decided they would drive over in Serena's Prius. On the way, they picked up June at her home. She was in her late sixties and still worked full time at a grocery store. She'd asked for the day off to attend the wedding.

"Oh, this is so exciting," June gushed once she was settled in the vehicle. "I'm so glad for you, Patricia."

Serena drove to the hall and checked the time after parking. It was almost eleven. The four exited the vehicle with the flowers and walked to the entrance area of the hall.

"I'll go see if everything is ready," Serena said.

She went and peeked in the doorway into the common room. It was full of the residents and staff sitting at tables covered in gray table cloths. Each one had eight small plates, cutlery, napkins, and glasses around the edge and a posy of flowers set in a short vase as a centre piece. The Justice of the Peace was standing with Bert and Daniel against the far wall. When Serena waved, Bert nodded.

Serena walked back to her mother. "They're waiting for us."

"I can hear the wedding march," June said as the music wafted out into the hall.

Simone handed Patricia, Serena, and June each a bouquet of flowers and kept one for herself. They lined up in the hall. June walked through the doorway and started down the aisle that had been left between the tables. When she was half way, Patricia slipped her hands in her daughter's arms and the three began their walk. They stopped in front of the JP and Patricia let go of their arms before she walked up beside Bert.

The closest table had been left empty for the wedding party to sit at. Serena and Simone sat on two of the chairs. It also served for anyone in the wedding party who needed to sit down during the ceremony.

The JP began the formal procedure. "We are here for the marriage of Bert Alec Madden and Patricia Marie Reed-Bell. They have come together in mutual devotion to make their commitment for a future together. Love is the joy of a deep personal relationship. Marriage is a relationship of two people who commit themselves to each other and to building a future together. Patricia and Bert, this is a very special day in your lives. You are here in front of witnesses to be joined in the formal state of matrimony. It is assumed that those taking marriage vows have a desire for lifelong companionship and that they will support, help, and comfort each other in every circumstance in life. Bert Alec Madden, do you...."

"Stop! I object to this marriage!"

There was a cumulative gasp as everyone turned towards the doorway. A man with dark hair and short beard, and dressed in tan slacks, beige shirt, and brown jacket stood there, his hand in the air.

"Dalton!" Bert gaped at his son.

"I object to my father being taken in by this gold digger and her daughters!"

This set the room abuzz.

"What?" Serena looked from Bert to Dalton. What was Dalton doing here? Had he been invited at the last minute.

"You don't know what you're saying!" Simone jumped up.

Serena stood beside her. "Yes. Mom's not a gold digger!"

"Dalton." Bert took a couple of steps toward his son. "What's going on? What are you talking about?"

Dalton walked part way along the improvised aisle. "It's a good thing Aunt Marianne let me know about this quickie wedding. And since I doubt she's marrying you because she's pregnant, I can only assume she's marrying you for your money."

"That's preposterous," Patricia sputtered. "We're marrying for love."

Dalton looked at her then did a second take as recognition dawned. "You're that famous romance writer. I recognize you from your picture. My wife buys all your books."

"So, now you know she's not marrying me for my money," Bert said.

"Oh," Dalton blushed. "Right." He looked around the room at the faces staring

back at him. "I'm sorry to have interrupted."
He turned to leave.

"Stay," Bert said, his voice was almost pleading. "You're here anyway."

"Yes," Patricia said. "Please stay."

Serena could feel everyone in the room hold their breath while they waited.

Dalton hesitated. "Okay."

There was a united sigh as everyone let out their breaths.

Bert smiled. "Come and sit up here." He pointed to the empty seat beside Serena.

Serena and Simone slowly sat down. Serena glanced at Simone. She wasn't sure if she wanted this man, who had just called her mother a gold digger, sitting at their table but he was already pulling out a chair. She would have turned her back to him but then she would have missed the rest of the wedding.

The JP cleared his throat and continued with the ceremony. With no further interruptions, Patricia and Bert were married. They kissed among the clapping of the guests. The JP held up his hand.

"And for the blessing from an Apache Ceremony. Bert and Patricia, now you will feel no rain, for each of you will be shelter for the other. Now you will feel no cold, for each of you will be warmth to the other. Now there will be no loneliness, for each of you will be company to the other. Go now to your dwelling place to enter into the days of your togetherness. And may your days be good and long upon the earth."

Bert held out his arm and Patricia slipped her hand into it. Together they walked down the aisle with June and Daniel behind them. The couple had asked that no confetti or rice would be thrown, but nothing was said about the guests throwing balloons. They all pulled them out from under their chairs and sent them flying through the air towards the aisle.

Bert and Patricia laughed as they reached up and knocked them back to the residents at the tables. The four left the common room to sign the papers.

While the others continued hitting the balloons, there was an uncomfortable silence amongst the three at the head table. Serena decided not to say a word to Dalton. For him to yell that their mother was a gold digger without even meeting her was unforgivable. And the way Simone ignored him made her think that she felt the same.

The wedding party returned and walked over to the table. Another chair was found and everyone had to scrunch together to make it fit. Serena could feel Dalton's arm brush hers.

The catering staff came out with platters full of sandwiches and set them on the tables. They returned with bowls of pickles and olives, and plates of cheese and devilled eggs. There was constant chatter as the platters and plates were passed around, so the guests could pick what they wanted. Bert had bought some bottles of Champagne for those who wanted a drink and three different juices for those unable to have alcohol because of medication or personal choice.

Serena studiously ignored Dalton but Daniel sat on his other side trying to engage him in conversation. As Dalton answered his questions, they began to laugh together.

When the meal was over there was a tinkling of metal on glass and silence fell on the room. Bert stood up.

"We want to thank you all for coming and witnessing our marriage," Bert said. "It is a special day and having you here made it even more special. This is the only speech being given and I'll keep it short." He picked up his glass. "First of all, I want to make a toast to my new bride, a beautiful lady with a wonder sense of humour and a kind spirit.

"To the bride," everyone said and raised their glasses.

"And to my new daughters, Simone and Serena. I look forward to spending time with both of you."

Again everyone raised their glasses.

"And lastly to my son Dalton who, though he made a spectacular entrance, is most welcome here with all of us."

Serena saw that Dalton at least had the decency to turn red as, for a third time a toast was made. Bert sat down and Patricia stood.

"I'm a writer and used to writing long winded speeches in my books." She held up her hand in the midst of groans. "But I only have a couple of things to say. I'd like to thank June and Daniel for standing up with us and witnessing our union. And I want to thank Bert for asking me to be his wife. I only see happy times ahead of us."

The guests clapped as Patricia sat down. The catering staff entered and began to clear off the tables. The lunch was over.

"I think we should move," Serena said to Simone as the residents started to come over to offer their best wishes. "They don't want to talk with us."

They stood and picked up their glasses of Champagne then walked over to stand beside the piano. They talked as they watched the residents drift away to their rooms or begin a pool game or sat to play cards. Everything was back to normal.

"Excuse me." They hadn't noticed Dalton approach them. "I really want to apologize for my behaviour today. It was an unthinkable thing to do and I'm very embarrassed."

"I think you should be saying that to my mother," Simone said coldly.

"I already have and I will continue to do so for the next ten years. It just sounded as if Dad was being railroaded into a wedding and I wanted to make sure it wasn't happening. I wanted to protect Dad and I couldn't think of anything else to do except show up today. I wanted to make sure no one was taking advantage of him."

"That's understandable." Serena looked at Simone. "We did just as bad, but not in front of such a large audience. We hired a detective to look into your dad."

"You what?"

"Like you, we wanted to protect our mother. But unlike you, when Mom found out about it, we were in deep trouble. She didn't take it well and the only reason she let it go was because your dad asked her to marry him."

"So we are all untrusting people," Dalton grinned.

"I'd like to call it loving our parents," Simone told him.

"And obviously, we do." Dalton looked at his watch. "I have to go, but I would like it if we could get together soon. For not only do you now have a brother, you also have a sister-in-law, two nieces, and a nephew."

"We would like that," Serena said.

Serena and Simone set their glasses on the piano and they exchanged phone numbers with Dalton.

"We will be having Christmas dinner at our place," Dalton said as he put his phone away. "If you want to come."

Serena looked at Simone. "We have to wait and see what Mom's plans are."

"Well, I'm going to ask them now so hopefully they will agree."

They said their goodbyes and Serena and Simone watched as Dalton went over to their mother and stepfather. He hugged them both and they could see Bert and Dalton wipe the tears from their eyes.

"Looks like we're going to be one big, happy family," Serena said.

"And mom is getting grandchildren, something we have failed to give her. Takes the pressure off us, especially since neither of us is in any kind of trivial relationship, let alone a serious one."

"Yes, it looks like Mom is the only one of us who will have a date this New Year's Eve."

Serena picked up their glasses from the piano and handed Simone's to her. "And we are back to both of us being single."

Simone clinked her glass to Serena's. "The Single Bells together again."

The End

Joan Donaldson-Yarmey's books published by BWL Publishing Inc.

Canadian Historical for Adults and Young
Adults
Rushing the Klondike
Romancing the Klondike
West to Grande Portage
West to the Bay

Mysteries
Sleuthing the Klondike
Gold Fever
The Travelling Detective Series

Holiday Romance

Joan Donaldson-Yarmey and Gwen Donaldson

The Twelve Dates of Christmas

BWL Author Gwen Donaldson

Gwen Donaldson was born and raised in Edmonton, Alberta Canada. She became a hairstylist after completing a beautician's course in High school and worked in a salon as well as doing hair for television stars. She moved to Toronto where she changed careers and registered to take a Travel Counselling Course at the Canadian Travel School. After completing the course she was asked to be their receptionist. She quickly became Manager of Student Services then went on to the head office as the National Manager of Human Resources for nine campuses across Canada. When Head office moved to Vancouver Gwen went along with it. There she and another manager did a manager's buy out and renamed the school the Canadian Tourism College. After 32 years in business Gwen and her partner sold the college and retired. She now enjoys travelling, spending time with family and friends, and writing holiday romances with her sister, Joan. Single Bells is the second one they have written together. The first was The Twelve Dates of Christmas

Joan Donaldson-Yarmey was born in New Westminster, B.C., Canada, and raised in Edmonton, Alberta. Over the years she worked as a bartender, hotel maid, cashier, bank teller, bookkeeper, printing press operator, meat wrapper, gold prospector, warehouse shipper, house renovator, and nursing attendant. During that time she raised her two children and helped raise her three step-children.

Since she loves change, Joan has moved over thirty times in her life, living on acreages and farms and in small towns and cities throughout Alberta and B.C. She now lives in Edmonton with her husband and one cat.

Joan began her writing career with a short story, progressed to travel and historical articles, and then on to travel books. She called these books her "Backroads" series and in the seven of them she described what there is to see and do along the back roads of British Columbia, Alberta, the Yukon, and Alaska. She has now switched to fiction writing and is proud to be one of Books We Love Ltd published authors.

Rushing the Klondike, Romancing the Klondike, West to the Bay, and *West to Grande Portage* are Joan's four Canadian Historical novels for adults and young adults.

She has had three mystery novels, *Illegally Dead, The Only Shadow in the House,* and *Whistler's Murder* published in what she calls the "Travelling Detective Series". They come in a boxed set. In her stand-alone novel, *Gold Fever,* she combines mystery with a little romance. *The Twelve Dates of Christmas* is a holiday romance.

https://www.bookswelove.com/donaldson-yarmey-joan/

http://thetravellingdetectiveseries.blogspot.com/

https://www.facebook.com/writingsbyJoan

.